P9-BIG-694

A Measure of Dust

a novel by

STEVEN TURNER

SIMON AND SCHUSTER / NEW YORK

Copyright © 1970 by Clarence Steven Turner

Published by Simon and Schuster
Rockefeller Center, 630 Fifth Avenue
New York, New York 10020

Second printing

SBN 671-20552-8
Library of Congress Catalog Card Number: 70-107260
Designed by Edith Fowler
Manufactured in the United States of America
by American Book–Stratford Press, Inc.

for my brother Cal
because of him I had to write

Like as a father pitieth his children, so the
Lord pitieth them that fear him.
For he knoweth our frame; he remembereth
that we are dust.
Psalms 103:13–14

ONE

THE MORNING it all started I was sitting at a table in the dining room at Wesley Academy having an argument with John Poole. It's funny that when a person is sitting down here in Jackson it makes Wesley seem a million miles away, but like the school catalog says it's really located "a hundred miles north of Jackson in the beautiful pinehill section of Choctaw County, Mississippi, eight miles from McCool, which is served by Tri-State Bus Lines and a branch of the Gulf, Mobile, and Northern Railroad." Of course, the catalog does not mention the fact that there are only two buses a day coming south and that the railroad up that way has no passenger service at all. And the roads are so bad in some places that even when you travel in a brand-new 1936 automobile it takes almost four hours to get there.

Anyway, that morning John Poole, who roomed with my brother Carl and me, was saying that just because Louis beat Max Baer last fall didn't mean a thing. He said that Schmeling would be smart and in condition, but I didn't possibly see how Schmeling could win if Baer couldn't. After all, old Maxie Baer had bounced that big Primo Carnera all over the ring.

At the head of our table Miss Hunter, crinkling her mouth into lines that looked like painted cat whiskers, rolled her eyes to indicate that she expected unruly conduct and loud arguing from John but not from me. So even though I wanted to argue some more, I didn't. Miss Hunter must have been about sixty years old, and she didn't really teach, she just kept study hall in the auditorium during the days. She had been having a pretty bad time lately. Somebody had found out that the low ceiling with the white recessed squares wasn't wood or beaverboard, it was tin. All spring in my afternoon study halls when things got very quiet and Miss Hunter herself was looking out the window or maybe reading, some smart boy would thumb a piece of chalk against that tin ceiling. Of course it would make everybody jump, that sudden *whang* in the quiet room. Miss Hunter's white face would turn very pinkish, and she would ask the guilty party to be a man and acknowledge his guilt. But the guilty parties never would. Once, when I got egged on by Allison McGee, I hit the ceiling with some chalk, too. But when Miss Hunter asked the guilty party to stand up, I couldn't help myself. I stood up.

She took me into the Bible Room right outside the auditorium. After looking at me for a minute, she said, "Not you, not you too, Mark?" It made me feel like Brutus must have felt when he stuck that dagger into Caesar. Then she said, "Oh, Mark, I could just cry." I thought she was maybe going to. So I said, "Gosh, Miss Hunter, I'm sorry. I didn't mean to hurt your feelings." She was looking away from me. I clutched her sleeve to get her attention. I was about to cry myself. Then she turned and kissed me on the cheek very quickly. She said that God had given me lots of talent, but that creating disturbances in study hall wasn't one I should develop. She thanked me for admitting what I'd done, suggesting that I might have set an example for others to follow. I sort of doubted that, but I didn't say anything as she picked up the yardstick from the blackboard. I turned around and leaned over. She hit five awful resounding whacks on the top of the desk. She smiled at me and we went back into study hall. The first chance he got to talk, John Poole said, "That burning butt is what you deserve for being a noble bastard."

My example really didn't inspire anybody either, especially the older boys. They even started bringing in rocks, pretty good-sized ones, and those things really made a racket when they hit. They also started to make some very noticeable dents in the ceiling. It got so bad that one night 'Fessor King came into night study hall—where all the junior and senior high boys were, the girls studying in their dormitory rooms—and he said he was not only going to beat the first rock thrower he caught until the guilty boy couldn't stand up but he was also going to expel him. That cooled them down. 'Fessor King never made any idle talk. He was the principal of the high school division, he taught Latin and mathematics, and he was in charge of the Square, the boys' dormitory that was shaped sort of like an old fort up on the top of the hill. The 'Fessor got plenty of respect from everybody—and not just because he used the paddle.

Well, that morning about the time John started arguing some more, I saw Reverend Ingram getting up from his table over near the dining hall entrance. The dining hall is really the basement of the girls' dormitory, Virginia Hall. Whenever the older boys are being nasty they always call it Virgin Hole, but the basement does make a nice dining hall, cool even on really hot days. On Saturday nights the boys date the girls in the dining hall; they sit and talk for two hours. Sometimes, if the chaperon doesn't watch too close, they can grab each other's hands, but not much else. Miss Hunter was supposed to be one of the toughest chaperons when she had that Saturday night duty. I remember hearing Bob Durham, about the most foul-mouthed boy in the dorm, say something about her being an old bitch. I asked why. He said, "She'd rather see you roast in hell than get a feel from one of those chickens."

Even though Mr. Ingram was a minister his face was deeply tanned from always working out in the open—chopping wood, running the saw, and even plowing sometimes. His eyes in his tanned face looked like two solid black marbles stuck in the side of a red clay bank. Now he seemed to stare out over the dining hall before he tapped the little bell at his table. As we all started to bow our heads he cleared his throat and said, "Mark Torrance will please stop and see me as he leaves the dining hall."

Then he prayed. The morning prayer was usually short and snappy, maybe a little longer on Sundays than on the other days of the week. Although the blessing was asked before every meal, there was no prayer at noon. But Mr. Ingram made up for it by really praying after supper; one time he went for twenty minutes.

As soon as Mr. Ingram said "Amen," about a hundred chairs slid back against the dark, heavily oiled floor. I had never been told to stop and see Mr. Ingram before. John Poole smiled at me and whispered, so Miss Hunter couldn't hear, "What the hell did you do now?" I was worried about Daddy and Mama down in Jackson, but I could see my brother Carl standing by the door as the other boys pushed out of the hall. If the folks were sick or something, I felt sure Mr. Ingram would have asked both of us to stop.

As I got to the main table Mrs. Ingram and her daughter Betty Ruth (that all the older boys called Baby) excused themselves. Mr. Ingram told me to sit down.

I waited while he stirred his coffee and stared across the dining room. He had a staring habit. Sometimes in church during his sermon I would get the feeling while he talked that he was staring through everybody there. Other times I would feel even worse, thinking he was staring right especially at me. I kept thinking about black marbles in a red clay bank.

While he was staring this morning I looked at the table very cautiously. I noticed a letter addressed to Carl Torrance, Sr. I just glanced at it, I didn't want him to think I was nosy, and then I stared, too, out beyond the entrance where I could see Carl waiting with John.

Finally Mr. Ingram said, "Well, I have some good news for you, Mark."

I smiled, still not knowing what to say.

"Your teachers tell me that you've averaged above ninety in all your courses. You're exempt from taking any final examinations."

He talked very solemnly like he was reading the text for the

Sunday morning sermon, but the news wasn't any real surprise to me. I knew what my average was. In fact, I had already started in my mind to enjoy that week of pleasure I had coming up. While all the others, most of them at least, suffered in those hot classrooms taking exams I was going to walk out to the lake, take nice cool swims, and stop in some sweet pine-scented woods on the walk back and practice my declamation so I could win that little gold medal next Monday, Commencement Day.

Feeling his eyes on me, I smiled. "That's sure good to hear, sir. I hoped I would be exempt."

He nodded at me. "You have a week until the declamation contest. How would you like to go home?"

I hadn't even given that a thought. Mama and Daddy had been living in Jackson at the end of the past summer, but when Daddy got a chance for a few months' work in Memphis, they asked Carl and me if we wanted to go to school at Wesley Academy. That way we boys could stay in one school without transferring Lord knows where—the way Daddy was having to hustle around looking for work. Carl and I really wanted to go, to get off and be on our own. Of course, it cost twenty-one dollars apiece for Carl and me each month—not counting a couple dollars for both of us to spend—but Mama said it would be worth it to know that we were in a fine Presbyterian school like Wesley. Carl and I were homesick for almost a month after we left, but we did get over it. Mother and Daddy had stayed in Memphis several months, and even when Carl and I went up there for the Christmas holidays we had missed Wesley. Memphis just wasn't our town the way Jackson was; it was too big a place for a boy to try to learn in two weeks. Anyway, Daddy had finished his Memphis work, and now the folks were back in Jackson living in an apartment that Carl and I hadn't even seen yet.

When Mr. Ingram cleared his throat very noisily, I looked at him and spoke up quickly, "It would sure be nice to go down to Jackson, sir, but I . . ."

As my voice started trailing off into nothing, I noticed the jaw muscles working under that brown skin. He must have put talcum powder on after he shaved that heavy black beard this morning; there was a funny chalky look on top of the brown skin. "Most boys," he said slowly, "would jump at the chance to get away from here a week early."

He was right about that. I'll bet I could name ten or fifteen personally that, as far as that goes, would have been glad to leave and never come back.

"It would be nice, sir, but . . ." I hated to say it, but finally I had to. "I don't have any money yet to go home on."

The folks hadn't sent us bus fare yet, but it was still a week until Commencement. Since the coming Saturday would be the first of June, I knew that within two or three days now Carl and I would be getting a check for three or four dollars—bus fare and a little extra. By the time we cashed the check and it got back to the bank in Jackson, there would be money to cover it because—whether Daddy was working or not—he would have fifty dollars on the first, his government compensation check. The First of the Month was always a big day in our lives.

Still, even if they had already sent the money, I don't think I would have seriously considered going about a hundred miles home just to turn around and come back after a week. I wanted to see the folks again, sure, but it would be a waste of money because I was going to be with them all summer.

His voice was solemn again. "Don't you and Carl have any money at all?"

"Well, sir, what we have at the present is only about seventy-five cents. The folks haven't sent our bus fare yet. And we owe Mattie a quarter of that. Our washwoman, Mattie, the one—"

"Yes, yes, Mark. I know Mattie."

Of course he should know her. She wasn't anything great as a washwoman; plenty of others who came up to the Square and took boys' washing in were better. But Mattie was famous. She always walked with a box of fresh wash balanced on her head. She had walked four miles in from the country with as much as fifty pounds of freshly done clothes balanced in a big cardboard box on top of her head. That may not be any world's record, but we were all proud of her, even the other washwomen.

"How old are you, Mark?"

"I was thirteen last month, sir."

"Is that all? And you're not really a big boy for thirteen, are you?"

I certainly knew that he knew how old I was. Last fall when Carl and I came up with the folks, there had been a kind of hassle about me being too young to enter the ninth grade. Finally Mr. Ingram said it would be all right, since my grades from the school in Jackson were very high. But they couldn't get straight why I was so young in such a grade. Mama finally said that I had skipped two grades in grammar school because I was very intelligent, but the truth was that I hadn't skipped any grades at all. Mama had just decided to start me in the first grade when I was four and a half; that way, she said, I could get help from Carl, who was eighteen months older and also starting to school. The real funny thing was that, after the first grade, Carl and I were never in the same room. He never got to help me much at all, which was just as well. Carl played around too much and didn't seem to care whether he learned anything or not. He also had a rougher gang of kids in his room. Just three years ago in the sixth grade, I remember, some older boy gave Carl a picture note to pass to Patricia Jones. The pictures were of a tin can, an eye, a screw, and finally the letter U. Pat gave the note to her teacher. There was quite an investigation in which some of the older boys in that class not only admitted to the principal that they had dated girls—in the dirty sense— but they had even bragged about it.

It happened that the summer before that investigation Carl and I and Haley Barber had taken a girl about our age into a vacant house in Jackson. This girl, Mary Catherine, had taken off her drawers, saying she would give each one of us a date. She made the other two stand in the corners and turn their backs while one of us was on top. The two uninvolved boys then counted to ten just as fast as they could. That was it; the date was over. I guess it had been exciting, but I didn't really see much to it. Mary Catherine enrolled in Daily Vacation Bible School a few days later, Carl and Haley and I started playing baseball almost every day—so we never really had any more dates with Mary Catherine. But when those older boys were making their confessions that day, Carl felt he had to speak up and sound like he'd had some experience himself. Fortunately, he did not mention that I was also involved with Mary Catherine that day. Later that night, after Daddy had given him a good whipping, Carl came out on the back porch, all crying and mad. He said I'd better be careful, that the folks thought I was so pure and all, but if I ever crossed him up he was going to tell on me. For a couple of years after that, every time I did something he didn't like, he would always say, "Okay, keep it up, keep it up. I'm going to tell Mama and Daddy something about you." But he never did tell, no matter how mad he got. Now I didn't think he ever would, although I still worried about it sometimes.

When Mr. Ingram stopped staring this time, he said, "Thirteen, are you, Mark? Exempt on your subjects, all finished with junior high. If you don't have the bus fare, you can still go home."

I started to say that I sure didn't want to borrow any money, but he kept right on talking. "Yes, Mark, I'm going to let you hitchhike to Jackson."

Only the older boys were allowed to leave school hitchhiking, and most of them had to have written notes from their parents saying they could do it. Mr. Ingram smiled as though I was the luckiest boy in the world, so I smiled too. I did feel pretty proud. And I was starting to think of other things, things that had been buried out in nowhere for months and months—the smell of that dark coffee Mama perked every morning, a couple of eggs for breakfast, maybe a piece of steak on Saturday nights (if Daddy was working), fig preserves on hot buttered toast, and real honest-to-goodness cane syrup with the biscuits—instead of that watery sorghum that was served in the dining room at Wesley. I could almost feel the crisp, clean bed sheets, hear Mama's laugh, and smell the mellow smoke from my daddy's Roi Tan cigar on Saturdays (if he had been working that week).

"Could I leave right away, sir?"

"Floyd Rollins takes the mail to McCool in about fifteen minutes. You might catch him if you hurry."

"Yes sir."

He picked up the letter and handed it to me. "Give this note to your parents. They'll be wondering why you came home this week."

"Oh, you explained to them about me being exempt."

"Yes, Mark." For a few seconds he looked me full in the face, and then he shook his head slowly. "Is your father working now, Mark?"

"I don't really know, sir. I honestly don't think he's done anything since they got back from Memphis right before Easter."

He looked toward me again, but this time past me, the way he would stare beyond the audience in church. "You boys' bill hasn't been paid in two months. I've told them the school will have to have eighty-four dollars—right away."

"Oh. Yes sir."

"There must be some way your father can get the money. You tell him it's a matter of whether or not you boys can stay in school."

"Yes sir. I'll give them the letter."

"Talk to them too. The school has to have its money. Well, hurry along now, Mark. Don't forget to practice that declamation. We expect big things from you next Monday."

My face was red, and I decided that the biggest thing he expected would be eighty-four dollars. But I shook his hand and hurried out of the dining hall. While I ran up to the Square with John and Carl, I didn't tell them anything except that I was getting to go home a week early because I was exempt.

A lot of boys gathered in the room watching me pack, all

talking about how lucky I was to get away like that. Carl didn't say much until the school bell started ringing at five of eight and the other boys left the room. John Poole waited at the door a minute, but Carl told him to go ahead, that he would catch up with him.

When John left, Carl said, "I just don't follow what this is all about."

There was just no use in my telling him something that would worry and embarrass him all week. Maybe for nothing. I mean, if Daddy got the money, then the bill would be paid and Carl wouldn't ever even know about it.

I said, "There's nothing for you to follow. I'm going home—like I said. We both knew I was going to be exempt."

"Yeah, yeah." He looked like he was going to say something else, but he had a science exam starting in a few minutes. He stood there, looking a little embarrassed, watching me finish packing that sweet-smelling little brown grip of Daddy's. Finally he said, "Be careful, Legs."

Ever since a year ago when he read something in *True Detective* about a guy called "Legs" Diamond, he had been calling me "Legs." I did have pretty sturdy looking calves, even though I was still pretty small myself.

I said there wasn't anything to worry about, that I could make it home all right. He tried to make me take all the seventy-five cents, but finally he kept twenty cents for himself to spend. Then he said, "Watch yourself on the road. Don't think you're grown-up all of a sudden. Be careful."

He grabbed my right hand, squeezed it hard, and then ran down the hill to catch up with John.

I walked out to the road and found a place where Floyd would be able to see me before he got up a lot of speed. I sat the grip down carefully so that white-yellow dust of the road wouldn't pop up around it too much. Even though the spring had been pretty dry, the air that morning was crisp and clear. There hadn't been much breeze or traffic to stir the dust. Despite all this worrisome business about the money, it felt good to know that I was through with school for three months now—in fact, through with junior high for keeps.

Waiting for Floyd was as good a time as any to practice my declamation, standing there on the road with no one around me. The speech was called "Ropes"—very much against capital punishment.

I said, "Ladies and gentlemen, let us conceive of time itself as being personified in the form of a huge clock which we have with us here in this auditorium. Let us turn our clock back almost two thousand years and imagine ourselves in the Colosseum of Rome. On the blood-drenched sand in the arena below there lies a warrior—terrified, pleading, the fear of death in his eyes. At his throat there is a sword, and behind that sword the brawny arm of a gladiator. The fallen warrior turns his face up to the crowd, but on those thousands of faces there is nothing of sympathy and pity, nothing but wild ferocity and a lust for the sight of blood. Their thumbs point toward the earth. 'Kill him!' they scream. 'Kill him!' He sinks back, dies, and the crowd shrieks with delight."

I saw Floyd's bright-red Ford V-8 making the curve, kicking up dust. I pointed my thumb toward the sky.

TWO

FLOYD ROLLINS always looked as if he was in complete charge of everything around him. I looked at him behind the wheel of that red Ford—a great big blond-headed guy who wasn't, I guess, all that old. I know that some folks still talked about how good a football player he'd been for Wesley three or four years ago. Since he was all that good supposedly and so big too, I didn't see why he wasn't playing now for Ole Miss or Mississippi State or maybe even for L.S.U. A lot of the older boys had been saying recently that L.S.U. wouldn't have a good team anymore since Huey Long was dead. I didn't know too much about Mr. Long, although I had seen him once when he led the L.S.U. band up Capitol Street in Jackson when the Tigers came to play Ole Miss during the state fair about two years ago. They really played them too—beating our team something like 50-0. I remember when Mr. Long was heading up Capitol Street waving a baton, not really twirling it, he looked like a man made to live, to get all the kicks he could from life. When he got shot last summer, I was a little concerned and certainly surprised, but nobody seemed to have any idea at first that he was going to die. I personally just never thought of a man like him dying. Just by accident I was down at the loading ramp behind the Jackson *Daily News* when the extras started rolling saying that Mr. Long was dead. I sold quite a few papers, made myself almost two dollars that day, but it was a sad thing. I don't know which was the worse day—Huey Long dying or Wiley Post and Will Rogers being killed in that Alaska plane crash. Both those bad days came pretty close together.

Floyd Rollins sort of reminded me of Huey Long in the way of being very sure of himself. I guess he had reason to be since he had a good United States Mail job, a snappy red Ford V-8, and a reputation for always having some good-looking little piney woods girl on the seat beside him.

Right now he didn't look too happy about putting me on that front seat. He glanced at me as the Ford stopped, stirring the white-yellow dust. He said, "What's that thumb in the air supposed to mean? You want me to take you to McCool for nothing, is that it?"

He didn't know how much I hated to ask folks for things or he wouldn't probably have said that. I knew that Floyd came up to the Square now and then and that some of the older boys ran around with him, but I didn't want to take advantage of that. Being just a kid, I couldn't even pretend that he was a friend of mine. He'd probably never even noticed me.

I said, "I'd sure pay you fifty cents if I had it, Floyd. But I'm going down to Jackson and I'm almost broke."

He leaned over, looking at me. "How much money you got?"

"Fifty-five cents. I had seventy-five, but I left my brother twenty cents to use for the week. And I really owe Mattie a quarter of this, but I'll pay her when I come back next Monday."

Floyd turned out his own window and shot some tobacco juice into the dust. He had very blue eyes that didn't seem to carry much expression—like one of the older boys in the dorm trying to keep a poker face when they played cards for cigarettes.

Floyd said, "Maybe you could give me the fifty cents when you come back Monday."

I had already thought about that. Maybe I could manage to get an extra fifty cents down at Jackson to pay him with when I came back, but it seemed awful to throw away money like that.

Fifty cents for an eight-mile trip! Why, a grown person could ride the Tri-State bus down to Jackson from McCool, almost a hundred miles, for a dollar and a half. And when I rode the bus from Memphis at Christmas I had gone for half-fare, even though I was over twelve then. Now that I was thirteen, of course, I wouldn't even be about to try to go half-fare. I hadn't wanted to at Christmas, but Mama had said that it wouldn't hurt to save money when you could. She also said that the bus company had more money than I did. That was certainly true, but it still didn't make it right. Finally, she said that the bus was going to make the trip whether I rode or not and that they might as well be getting half a fare from me as have an empty seat that they got nothing for. That made a little better sense, but I was still embarrassed the way the bus driver looked at me and Carl back there when we got on in Memphis. Poor Carl will be fifteen in September, but as long as he doesn't get too big I suppose Mama will expect him to ride half-fare. Carl will probably start shaving pretty soon, and he's going to look funny as the devil trying to ride half-fare with a bearded face. The whole business is bad. I say that if there's a rule then a person should try to follow that rule.

So I hated to be a tightwad with old Floyd, but even though I had packed Daddy's fine sweet-smelling grip pretty solid, I think I would have walked the eight miles before I'd throw away money like that.

When Floyd saw me hesitating, all at once he reached out and opened the door on my side. "Put your grip on top of that mail sack."

"Look, Floyd, I—"

"Hell, get in. You can pay me in a few years when you're building privies for the WPA."

I mumbled some kind of thanks, put my grip in the car, and sat down. As we started rolling, Floyd said, "You heard that joke, didn't you, about the privies?"

I said I didn't know for sure.

"Man calls the WPA out to do a job for him, says he wants

two men sent out to hoe his field for a day. Well, he's not out at the field when the men show up, but the WPA sends eight. First thing, they build a privy. Later on, the farmer comes out, says he sent for only two men, so why's there eight out there and who the hell built a privy on his property? The WPA boss says, 'Two men to work. You sent for two. That's what you got.' The other guy says, 'Eight. I counted eight.' The boss says, 'Yeah, that figures right. Two coming, two going, two shitting, and two hoeing.' "

Floyd laughed and slapped his thigh. Actually I had heard the story from somebody else—probably that filthy Bob Durham. I guess it's funny but it's also uncouth. I certainly wouldn't tell it unless I changed the words a little. I laughed some when Floyd did, but I sure hoped he wouldn't start telling dirty stories. Just last month, the evangelist John Gabriel had been at Wesley for a week. I had made a few pledges about my conduct, and I hated to sit in the ways of the wicked. Not that I could exactly help myself in the present situation. I could either ride in that bright red Ford or else get out and walk to McCool.

But I needn't have worried. Floyd got quiet again. As we wound along the narrow road, he beeped his horn now and then at a farmer plowing in the dust or maybe an old lady sitting by herself on one of those weathered unpainted front porches. But after we got way down the road from Wesley I could hardly see houses at all—almost none, in fact, close to the road. Most of the time it was just that red-yellow clay road, sometimes cut through high red banks, between the thick green pine trees and the honeysuckle vines and the weeds. It made me seem far away from everything, especially moving along pretty fast like that. I thought Floyd was a little careless, the way he'd get on the wrong side of the road sometimes on a curve so he wouldn't have to cut his speed. But I didn't say anything. I drove a tractor at school for a few minutes a couple of times, but I never did anything with an automobile but steer it whenever Daddy would let me practice.

Suddenly Floyd shot a stream of tobacco juice out his window. Going pretty fast the way we were, I felt very sure that some of that spray had circulated in the breeze over to my side. I really wanted to take out my handkerchief and put it over my face like some kind of doctor during an operation, but I thought Floyd might be insulted. Instead, I sort of easily sneaked my hand up to my face and covered my nose and mouth whenever he spit. He probably just thought I was scratching my nose.

Floyd said, "Which one of the Torrance boys are you?"

"Mark. Carl's my brother."

"I know. I remember you boys played some junior football before the big games last year. You both played end, ain't that right?"

"We played some, but not much. Neither one of us was big enough—even for junior football."

"You'll stretch out some and pick up the meat later on. But you both played that end spot good. I like the way you come in wide on the defense. I never saw a runner get outside either one of you."

"Thanks a lot, Floyd." Coming from a well-known Wesley star who could have gone to Ole Miss and starred except that he got a good government job, this was about as fine a compliment as a boy could get for his football playing.

Pretty soon Floyd spit again. Then he glanced over my way. "How come you're leaving Wesley now when school don't let out for a week?"

I told him that Reverend Ingram had said I could go because I was exempt.

Floyd sort of shook his head. "That's mighty unusual."

"Oh, no. There were about three others in school that were exempt."

"I mean unusual he let you go home. The old devil wouldn't go out of his way to give a man ice water in hell. The fact is, more I think about it, if he caught you with ice water in hell he'd take it away from you."

I wasn't feeling particularly good toward Reverend Ingram at the time, but I didn't laugh. I would just let it be on Floyd's own conscience to talk that way about an ordained man of God.

Floyd said, "I been thinking. You in a hurry to get to Jackson?"

I told him that I certainly was, that I was hoping to be there by the middle of the afternoon. If Daddy was working, Mama would have a nice supper, and if she hadn't fixed enough—since they weren't expecting me—they might even go out and buy me a nice little steak. I could remember a few years before, when things were really bad, almost nobody working and all the men hanging round the poolrooms or sitting on benches in Poindexter and Smith parks, that some days all we had to eat at home was toast and coffee for breakfast and a few fried sweet potatoes the rest of the day. Sweet potatoes have a lot of minerals and energy, but a person can sure get tired of them after four or five days in a row. But, like I said, whenever Daddy was working, Mama always tried to make up for those bad eating days.

Floyd said, "That's too bad you in such a hurry. I got about an hour before I have to stop and drop this mail off in McCool. The damned bus is never on time, so I usually have about two hours."

I nodded, watching him spit out the window. He turned and winked at me.

I said, "Don't you get tired waiting so long around a place like McCool?"

"McCool ain't much, I'll say that. But it's a damned sight more than that cow turd in the road we just left. Two hundred twenty-three people."

"But that's not counting the Wesley students, the boarding ones. There's over a hundred of them."

"The thing is, Mark, I don't just hang around McCool. I got this little insurance business on the side. I don't mention it too much because the government don't want its employees making money on the side. I got to stop and see a lady right now on business. Her old man goes to work up in Weir and she's there in the house by herself except—"

"What does her daddy do?"

"Not her *daddy*—her old man, her husband! He's working for the damned dairy at Weir."

"Oh! Her husband."

"The thing is my little lady customer has a kid around the house. When we talk business, the kid gets in the way, don't you understand?"

I nodded.

"That's where you could sure be handy if you wasn't in such a hurry. You could take care of the kid."

I laughed. "That's pretty good, Floyd—me taking care of somebody's baby. I wouldn't know what to do."

"Jesus, the kid's a fourteen-year-old gal! You could walk her out in the woods. Nice warm morning like this."

He started slowing the car. Down the road was a little frame white house set back about thirty yards under the pine trees. Floyd stopped the car by the mailbox. He said, "Uncle Sam's postman got to make a pickup." That started him laughing so hard he almost swallowed his tobacco wad. He reached over with his left hand and put the tin flag down. Then he opened the mailbox. I was surprised because this was the first time he'd stopped to collect mail.

All he pulled out was a small piece of white paper. He glanced at it for a second, then he stuck the paper in his mouth and chewed hard for a minute. He leaned over the side of the car and spat the whole wad, tobacco and paper and all, out into the dust.

He said, "Well, how about it?"

"What?"

"You got time to help me out for an hour or so? The kid's been out of school sick for damned near a week. It cramps hell out of my business conversation."

"I—I really ought to get on down to Jackson, Floyd."

"Hell, we won't be here an hour. Look at it this way. If you'd had to walk you wouldn't hardly be a mile from Wesley by now."

"I reckon that's the truth."

"You might have yourself some fun." He leaned over with a big grin and tapped his finger on my chest. "Baby, that kid has got some nice titties on her."

"Gosh, Floyd, I'm really pretty little. The girl probably won't even talk to me."

"You're big enough all right. All you have to do is think big. Why, I've got ass that I never dreamed of getting—just because I decided to go after it."

"I just don't know, Floyd. She might not even talk to me."

"All right, the worse comes to the worst she's got a Monopoly set at the house. That Geraldine's a whiz at Monopoly. She'll give you a good fast game."

Well, of course, a person could always have a good time playing Monopoly. I might get embarrassed around the girl, but at least I wouldn't have to talk so long as we were throwing those dice and getting our properties bought. I knew that an hour wouldn't be much time. You could hardly get a good game going in an hour. But Floyd had saved me a long walk.

"Okay," I said. "But I'm just going to stay an hour, Floyd. I really have to get on down to Jackson."

He smiled, and punched me lightly on the shoulder. "That's the spirit, baby. You're gonna be a helluva football player too." He winked again. "Tell you something else. I'll bet you don't have to waste much time playing Monopoly either. That little gal looks like a chip off the old block. And titties! Jesus, I wish she was older."

While we were talking, the door of the house opened and a dark-haired woman in a white dress with blue polka dots came out. She waved her hand like she was telling us to come up the little road. Floyd gunned the car up to the house; then he turned and backed until the nose of the car was pointed out down the drive again.

He smiled at the woman, but he whispered to me. "A good

thing to remember, Mark. Whatever the situation is, always keep your transportation headed so you can move out in a hurry."

The woman was acting as if she'd just noticed me. She wasn't really frowning, but she sure stopped her smiling all at once.

After we got out of the car we walked up on the porch.

Floyd said, "Morning, Mrs. Wester. Thought I'd stop and see you about that insurance policy this morning on my way to McCool."

She had a big false smile on her face, looking at me. "Who's the boy you brought with you, Mr. Rollins?"

"A young friend of mine on his way to Jackson. We can't stay long, Mrs. Wester. The United States mail has to get through, you know."

"Yes, indeed, Mr. Rollins. A person can always depend on the United States mail."

Floyd said, "My friend Mark says he don't mind us stopping here a bit while I take care of that insurance policy with you."

Mrs. Wester smiled, showing some very fine white teeth. She was really very good-looking. I wouldn't normally have thought she would have a fourteen-year-old daughter. Except that she had her eyebrows made too dark, she was a fine-looking woman.

Floyd said, "How's your daughter, Mrs. Wester? Is she well enough to be back in school?"

"No, Mr. Rollins, I don't think she'll go back for another day or two. She's still a mite puny, and the school is close to ending now anyway." She turned toward the front door. "Geraldine, come out and meet Mr. Rollins' nice friend."

I was a little nervous, not knowing what to expect, but in a few seconds this really wonderful-looking girl came out, dark-haired and dark-eyed, milky smooth white skin just like her mama. The light cotton dress she wore was very thin, and a person couldn't help noticing how rounded this girl was up at the chest. Old Floyd had sure been right about that.

Floyd said, "Geraldine, this is Mark."

She said, "Hi, Mark," and then sort of studied me for a few seconds. "How old are you?"

"Thirteen."

She looked like she'd swallowed a forkful of sour turnip greens. Well, Floyd couldn't blame me. I had tried. The thing is that a girl just doesn't like to fool with a kid younger than she is.

Her mother said, "Listen, Geraldine, why don't you children go outside and find some kind of play while me and Mr. Rollins discuss my insurance policy?"

Geraldine rocked her hip back against the door with her chest high in the air. "There's nothing to do, Mama."

This seemed to stump Mrs. Wester. She looked at Floyd just like she'd tried some of those same sour turnips Geraldine had spit out. Geraldine didn't bat an eye, leaning against the door looking at them—but not paying me any attention. Well, you couldn't blame a husky good-looking girl for not looking at me.

We just stood there, the four of us about like four different cars that come up to a street intersection at the same time—all of us stopped, afraid we would bump the other if we moved first.

I said, "Say Geraldine, I hear you've got a Monopoly game."

Floyd smiled and nodded to Mrs. Wester. She slapped her hands together and started bobbing her head like she was trying to out-nod Floyd. I started nodding, too. Our heads must have looked like apples strung up for Halloween.

Geraldine didn't say a word. And she never did nod. But after a few seconds she turned and went into the house. It wasn't but a second or two, and she was back with the Monopoly game under her arm.

Mrs. Wester said, "You children can have a fine game. Y'all find a nice place over in the pine grove, Geraldine."

"All right, Mama."

Mrs. Wester said, "I won't have you running back and forth in the house though—getting dust all over my Chinese carpet.

I'm going to lock my front door, I just won't have you tracking dust. You just play with Mark for a while, you hear me now, Geraldine?"

"I hear you, Mama."

"And don't be disturbing me every few minutes. I have to talk business with Mr. Rollins."

"Yes ma'am."

Geraldine started down the front steps from the porch, carrying the Monopoly set with her. As I started down after her, Floyd slapped me on the back. "You kids relax and have yourselves a little fun. Okay, Mark?"

He reminded me of a great big white cat with a fat catsup-covered sardine plunked right in its mouth. I nodded.

Floyd said to Mrs. Wester, "You wouldn't think it, 'cause that boy's still so small, so young. But he's gonna be a fine football player, you mark my word, Mrs. Wester."

She said, "Well, I would imagine so."

As I walked past the car, I wondered if Floyd ought to lock it. I'd sure hate for somebody to come along and steal my grip. The clothes in it didn't amount to much, but I would sure hate to tell Daddy that his sweet-smelling grip got stolen while I was sitting in the woods playing Monopoly. Then I decided I was worrying for nothing. If a man's grip is not going to be safe sitting right alongside the United States mail then it's not going to be safe anywhere.

Geraldine was long-striding about fifteen yards ahead of me toward a little cluster of pine trees beyond the hogpen. She had long white legs, and I hate to say that I was also watching her bottom twitch as she walked. I remembered what the evangelist John Gabriel said about the temptations of the flesh, and I looked up to the sky where a white cloud was drifting against the blue. I tried to think of a Scripture verse to arm myself with, but I couldn't seem to think of one that fitted the situation. I started looking at Geraldine's fine bottom again.

We sat down in the little group of pines. The air had the

spring smell of green pine needles, and the ground beneath the trees was covered evenly with the brown needles that had fallen before. It was still cool under the trees, even though there wasn't much breeze. Of course, any wind would have been bad because Monopoly money gets blown around so easy.

Geraldine set the game up very quickly, not looking at me at all for a while—acting like a grocery clerk with suspicions about a check Mama had sent me to cash. I mean she was just downright sullen.

I guess there isn't anything more fun than a good game of Monopoly. Speck Horner had been the first boy up at the Square to own a game back in the fall, and he made so much money renting it out for twenty cents a day that when everybody came back from the Christmas holidays at least four boys had brought sets back with them. So many sets kind of crowded the market, and Speck let it be known that he didn't appreciate one bit the others trying to take part of his business. With all the competition he did have to cut his renting price to fifteen cents a day; even at that, he told two freshmen who were trying to rent their sets that he'd beat hell out of them if they rented to any of his customers. Being freshmen, they were pretty scared and just stopped renting their sets entirely, because any time an upperclassman wanted to, he could tally them (five hard licks with a belt or coat-hanger) or make them fetch stove wood for his room or do any of a number of other chores.

Speck was also famous for devising the cruelest punishment of all. In January and February, when quite a few days stayed below freezing, Speck would send three freshmen crunching through the ice down to Room 31, the outhouse about fifty yards below the Square. The two toilets in Room 30 at the Square, regular flusher types, were always cut off when the weather was real cold in order to keep the pipes from breaking. Anyway, those three boys would have to sit down in Room 31 warming those cold damp seats, sometimes as long as half an hour, before Speck came down there. Another upperclassman asked Speck why he sent three boys since, after all, a person could only use one seat. But Speck said he didn't want to get too set in his ways, that he liked to have three choices before he finally made up his mind to sit down. He was generous too. Sometimes he would get a couple of upperclassmen to come down with him and use the extras that he had gotten warmed up.

Geraldine and I started playing Monopoly like we were out for real money. For about twenty minutes we just kept throwing those dice and buying all the property we could. She never said a word, but when I was throwing the dice or buying a deed of property, I would look up sometimes real suddenly and see her staring at me. Her bright dark eyes sort of stared me down too. I tried not to get outstared by a girl, but I couldn't help it. It was also a little embarrassing to me because I thought that she thought I was looking at those fine titties Floyd had mentioned. The fact is that sometimes I was looking at them. The skin of her face was white and clear too. I found myself wishing I was a couple of years older or at least a little bigger. I really wanted to make a good impression on her. The only thing that bothered me while she was playing Monopoly so fast and furious was this darned toothpick she'd dragged from her dress pocket and stuck in her mouth. While she was rolling the dice I'd glance at her. She had a nice soft-looking mouth, but that darned toothpick took something away from it. She wasn't really picking her teeth either, just chewing on the pick.

Finally she must have noticed me watching her. She said, "What are you staring so bug-eyed at?"

I wasn't a bit bug-eyed, but I was looking. "That toothpick."

"That's all it is—just a plain toothpick. Quit staring at it."

"Sure."

"What's wrong with my toothpick?"

"Nothing. And you're right. It is your toothpick. I don't have a thing to do with it."

"You want one?"

Now what would I want with one? Personally I don't believe

in chewing on toothpicks like that in public. But I said, "You got another one?"

"Not with me." She started to get up. "But I'll go up to the house and get a few."

"No, don't worry about it." I could just see her trying to bust into the house, interrupting that insurance discussion, making Floyd and her mama mad—all so she could pick up some toothpicks. I said, "I'll get one later. We have to play fast. We didn't have enough time for a Monopoly game to begin with."

She nodded. We threw some more dice and bought some more property. We had both taken four thousand dollars from the bank to begin with, instead of fifteen hundred, so as to speed up the property buying. But Monopoly is a funny game. There's an awful lot of luck involved, especially right at first. If a person happens not to land his token on the right places to buy good property during the first few runs around the board, then he might as well give up. And poor Geraldine was having awful luck with the dice. Not only had I thrown two doubles, getting an extra turn each time, but when she shot she always seemed to hit cheap property or Free Parking or Just Visiting in Jail or the railroad lines. The railroads are good property when a person gets them all, but she didn't have much else except Vermont and Connecticut avenues. Meantime, I had already sewed up the yellow and green corner from Atlantic to Pennsylvania Avenue, and I had even bought Park Place. I could see after twenty-five minutes or so that she was finding the game sort of boring. I couldn't say I blamed her. I wished the dice would stop being so lucky for me, but they wouldn't.

She threw a six and landed smack on North Carolina Avenue where I already had three houses. She rapped the thimble down hard when she finished counting the spaces.

I said, "That will cost you a thousand dollars."

I didn't gloat or anything when I said it, but all at once she moved her hand across the board and brushed all my houses into one pile right in the middle. She said, "Oh, pee-pee."

"What?"

"Pee-pee on this silly game."

In my whole life no girl had ever come out and said "pee-pee" right in front of me like that. Even though I could feel my face getting red, I gave her a hard look. She just looked right back.

I said, "You ought not talk like that."

"What grade are you in?"

"I just finished the ninth. I didn't have to take any exams at Wesley. I was exempt."

I believe that word *exempt* was sort of too much for her, but she nodded her head like she was impressed. "And you're not but thirteen years old?"

I nodded, but I was sure wishing I had told her I was fifteen. That way she wouldn't have felt that she had to be uppity with a boy younger than her. But then, small as I was, if I'd told her fifteen she'd probably have thought I was some kind of midget.

We just looked at each other for a while. I reached the point I couldn't put up with her anymore. I had collected the Monopoly money and stacked it in the box. I finished sorting the property cards.

When she saw me starting to stand up, she caught my right hand. "Don't leave yet."

Her hand was as warm and smooth as a cat's belly. But I said, "I have to go. We must have been here almost an hour. I have to get on down to Jackson."

"Don't go back to the house yet. They not through talking business yet."

I'll bet they were. Floyd was probably sitting there having a cup of coffee trying to sell that lady more insurance. You could figure a man like Floyd would keep selling just as long as he had something to put up on the market.

I started to shake my hand loose, but I didn't. I had a warm feeling and I looked at her chest again. I knew she knew I was looking, but right then I didn't care. I got on my feet, and she just made me pull her up at the same time, still holding onto my hand. When she got on her feet she stayed real close to me, her face on the same level with mine. If I wasn't taller than her, the way it ought to have been, at least she wasn't taller than me. She looked me right in the eyes.

I just couldn't keep looking at her like that. I started to pull my hand loose, but she wouldn't let me. Instead the next thing I knew she pulled my hand up and put it against one of her titties. Surprised like I was, I just let it stay there while the time just seemed to stop. I didn't squeeze or anything like that, but I couldn't help noticing how round and solid it felt. Then I turned and ran for the house.

I was almost to the front door when she caught me. I guess she could move those long white legs quick as the wind, because there she was, catching me from behind, pulling me back.

I said, "For gosh sake, turn loose!"

She said, "Ssh, hush. They'll hear you."

I didn't care if they did. I started to say something else, real loud this time, but she put her hand to my mouth. I pushed it away. Then, I couldn't help myself, I kind of spat too. Her hand tasted like dust.

She said, "Please don't make any noise. They're still busy."

"How do you know?"

I looked very close at her face. Her eyes were blinking, almost like she was going to cry. She bit her lip, and this time I did stare her down. I said, "Don't cry. I wasn't really running from you. I was just a little nervous."

I said that because I could see that she was hurt, even though she wasn't mad. I didn't want her to be mad. I remembered reading about Hell not having any fury like a woman scorned. I didn't want her to think I was scorning her. That wouldn't have been kind at all.

She took my hand. "If you don't believe they're still busy, come on. We'll go see."

She walked me around to the side of the house where there was a window. The shade was pulled down all the way, it seemed to me, so when Geraldine put her head up to the window I wondered how she could see anything. But she kept looking.

Finally I said, "Are they still talking?"

She turned and put her finger to her lips. Actually I had been whispering anyway.

She backed away from the window. "Look."

With my face against the screen and shading my eyes with my hands, I saw there was a narrow slit where the shade wasn't quite all the way down. After a person sort of adjusted his eye to the screen he was looking through, as well as the dim light inside, he could make out things in the room. It was a bedroom.

Geraldine whispered, "What's the matter? Can't you see?"

I saw all right. In that yellow-golden light that came from the sun hitting the back shade, I saw Floyd's butt moving up and down. And there were two feet running into two legs running into the woman I couldn't see at all; the legs just ran back under Floyd, like a man lying on his stomach with four legs like spokes running out from him. My face turned red. It seemed that something had kicked me in the stomach. I turned and ran again.

Geraldine caught up with me by the time I got to the pine grove. But she didn't say anything. I sat on the brown pine needles, just staring down, not knowing what to do. There were those red-brown needles, the soft sweet smell of the trees, and the bright blue sky. And then there was Floyd and Geraldine's mama hunching and rolling like those pigs wallowing in that pen back of the house. I just hadn't expected to see that. It wasn't that anybody had to tell me about any birds and bees. I just hadn't expected to see that.

Geraldine said, "You really run, don't you? Why don't you just walk sometimes?"

"We had no business sneaking up there like that."

But I was worrying suppose something happened at that dairy where her daddy worked and he came home without any warning. He would probably shoot so fast that Floyd would drop like one of those Indians falling from the saddle in a Buck Jones picture.

Geraldine said, "Did you ever do it?"

"What?"

"Do *it*?"

That time I understood her. "Yes."

"Honest?"

"I almost always tell the truth."

"When?"

"When what?"

"When was the last time you did it?"

"Oh, let's see." I didn't want to say that there had only been one time almost four years ago, and I certainly didn't want to provide any such ridiculous details as the fact I had stayed on top of Mary Catherine just long enough for Carl and Haley Barber to count ten as fast as they could. I still didn't know too much about the process, but it was obvious that it wasn't supposed to be that fast. Ten seconds is a lot of time, depending on the action; I mean, some people like this great Negro named Jesse Owens from Ohio can run a hundred yards under ten seconds. But this other business wasn't supposed to be done in such a hurry. Old Floyd was obviously not in any big hurry. We had been at that house almost an hour and he was still *there*.

I said, "The last time was a few months ago."

She said, "The boys and girls at Wesley don't get to mix together very much, do they?"

"Not much. They watch us pretty close."

She leaned herself back on the pine needles. I looked at her face, then started to stand up. But I didn't really know where I was going, and she caught my hand again. She was sure a hand-grabbing girl.

"Rest a little longer," she said. "Floyd's not ready to go yet."

I flopped my head back on the pine needles. She didn't say anything for a minute or two. I watched the little white clouds sailing along in the sky. I would spot them against the tops of the pines and in my mind I would tell them to be still, but they kept moving, sailing along. Then I thought about Floyd and that woman. My face started turning red again. I could feel it, but I hoped Geraldine wouldn't notice.

I kept thinking about a very nasty picture someone had drawn on the wall of Room 31, the outhouse below the Square. A very dirty drawing, a naked man and woman, legs spread and all that. Enough to make a person sick. I prayed several nights for the sick soul that drew that picture. It stayed on the wall a long time too, but finally when the evangelist John Gabriel was in the middle of his week-long revival somebody went down and scrubbed the wall clean.

Geraldine said, "A penny for your thoughts."

"I wasn't thinking. I was watching those clouds."

"Well, talk to me."

I hadn't practiced my declamation for a whole hour. There was a specially tough section for me toward the last of the speech. I could never seem to get it exactly right.

"Listen to this, Geraldine." I stood up, because when I'm saying that declamation I always get excited and it doesn't seem right to be lying down saying such strong things. I faced Geraldine and held my hands out, palms up. "Don't you see what I mean? Don't you see what I am driving at? Ladies and gentlemen, what are we to do with this wretched, desperate brother of ours who will not obey us though we lock him behind bars of iron, who will not love us though we whip him with a cat-o'-nine-tails, who will—"

"A cat with *nine* tails?"

She caught me right in the middle of my gesture. I dropped my hands. "It's a whip, that's all. A whip with nine knotted cords that really raises welts."

"My papa ought to have one of those. Then it wouldn't take him so long with his belt."

I turned away and looked toward the house. "I'm sorry he beats you."

"He's pretty mean. He's always worried some boy is going to screw me."

Good gosh! Just last night I had stood there in the middle of Wesley Presbyterian Church and delivered a short talk connected with the Save Our Youth program. Last night I was standing in a fine church delivering a talk like that, and this morning I was involved in fleshly sin up to my ears.

"I don't think you can blame your papa for that."

"You mean you think I'd let some boy screw me?"

"I didn't mean that. I mean that a papa is bound to worry about his daughter—especially a good-looking girl like you."

I kept staring at the house, wishing that Floyd would come on out of there. Well, in a way I wished he would, and in another way I really wasn't in a hurry anymore.

"Would you like to do it again?"

"Start on my speech?"

"I mean screw."

Every time she said that word it was like fingernails scraped across a blackboard. I turned around to her. She had dropped the left side of her dress down from her shoulder. Sitting in plain sight was this fine white titty with a small red nipple like the tip of a No. 2 Eagle pencil eraser. I admit that I had seen some titties in pictures, but not many. A lot of the older boys kept copies of *Esquire* magazine, because the Petty girls were pretty nice. But J. D. Stuckey always liked to go everybody one better. He came back from Greenville one weekend with a whole flock of nasty pictures that really showed titties. I never took but one look at them, but I remembered that time. And now here was the first honestly live titty I could remember seeing in my whole life.

Geraldine said, "Come here."

I walked over and looked down at that pink-topped white bump. She did have the whitest kind of flesh, sort of like the flesh that a girl shows when she first puts on a bathing suit in the summer. I sat down by Geraldine and looked at the titty.

She said, "You can touch it if you want to."

I was trying like the devil to think of a good Scripture verse to take all this off my mind, but I just couldn't seem to dig up one on short notice that was against good-looking titties. About the closest I came was the verse about beware of looking at the wine when it is red and sparkles in the glass. That verse didn't strengthen me very much, because wine was something that never had bothered me. But on days when I wasn't feeling very strong in the spirit, I had looked at some of those big-chested Wesley girls and I had lusted. I know it's all Satan's work, but there is something about titties that makes a boy want to rub his hand across them.

I reached out. When my fingers touched that pink spot, it crinkled like I'd seen the nipples on my own chest do when I jumped into icy water in the early spring. Geraldine's white skin got goose-bumpy too even though it was warm. She breathed fast, like she had jumped into icy water, too.

I was so hard it was embarrassing under my gray cotton trousers. But I didn't know what to do. I just kept my hand on the titty and moved my fingers around the nipple. She started breathing harder. Although I wasn't looking down below, when I felt her squirming with her arms and legs and tugging at something, I knew what she was doing.

She said, "Now. Look at that."

Down there was a small patch of shiny curly black hair, almost like some kind of strange dark affliction that had grown on her smooth white skin and that she would just have to put up with from now on. It was interesting and exciting and certainly about twice the size of the brown hair patch on me, but I kept wishing I was back at Wesley listening to John Gabriel or even to Reverend Ingram. It sure seems easier to be strong against temptation when the temptation isn't presenting itself more or less smack in your face.

She said, "Did you ever see anything like that?"

"Not really. Not exactly like that."

The truth was that when I stayed that ten seconds on top of

Mary Catherine I remember that she didn't have any hair at all, just all smooth round-bellied and bunched-up flesh down there. Of course, I didn't have any hair then either. In fact, I still didn't have too much (the older boys all said me and Carl would be late maturing), and I sure hoped Geraldine didn't want to take a look at mine. I had something down there all right, but compared to the rest of it the hair didn't amount to much.

It's a wonder she couldn't hear my heart whanging like a diving board vibrating nonstop. She took my hand. I had hoped that she would. Then she dropped it down right in the midst of that little clump of hair. It was coarser, more bristly than I thought it would feel, springing up around my fingers like it was charged with electricity.

"Move your fingers down a little lower," she said. "There, right there. Press it. Rub it."

I did. Against that warm and slick-soft part of her my finger moved and pressed. She breathed fast and hard through her mouth, like a football player who'd run eighty yards for a touchdown.

Just last night I was in church. I remembered the closing hymn.

> *Yield not to temptation, for yielding is sin.*
> *Each victory will help you some other to win.*
> *Fight manfully onward, dark passions subdue.*
> *Look ever to Jesus.*
> *He will carry you through.*

I took my hand away and jumped up so fast that for a few seconds she didn't know I had moved. She just lay there, her dark-lashed eyelids closed, her mouth tensed into an O shape. I turned away and looked up. The blue sky seemed to press down on me for my guilt in touching her that way, but I also felt another kind of guilt—a funny kind for getting up and leaving her like that. I glanced back to her, but I didn't want to shame her too much by looking.

43

Her eyes were open. "What's the matter, Mark?"

That was the first time she'd used my name since we'd been alone. It made me feel closer to her. I said, "I'm sorry. I just had no business touching you that way."

"I wanted you to."

"That doesn't make it right."

"You want to screw me. I can tell. Just look at you."

If it was possible, my face got redder. "Stop using that word. Just because a person wants to do something doesn't necessarily make it right. That's how Satan works. He makes us talk ourselves into sin."

"Don't be scared, Mark. Come back over here."

I looked at her, the dress back down from her shoulder again, those pretty white legs and belly and that dark hair.

"I'm sorry, Geraldine, I really am. But I just can't."

"I'll show you what to do."

I stood there, breathing now like I was the player who ran the eighty yards. There's a funny vein in my forehead that just pops up throbbing with blood when I'm excited. I put my finger up there and felt it pounding away. I knew I couldn't resist the temptation forever. I should have walked away so as not to have to look at it any longer. But I was standing there, like I'd turned into one of those pine trees.

Floyd Rollins' horn started blasting so loud the trees seemed to shake. I said, "Good gosh!" and then I turned and looked around one of the trees to see if Floyd could see Geraldine like that. But I was back of the tree and she was lying in that little hollow, so he couldn't really see either one of us.

The horn kept blasting. It's funny, but I wasn't hard at all anymore. Everything was scared right out of me. You might say Floyd was like a Heavenly messenger blowing that horn, but I guess that doesn't seem right either when you remember what I've just told about him. Anyway, Geraldine pulled her bloomers on right away and jerked her dress back over her shoulder. She seemed pretty disgusted.

I said, "Goodbye. I'll see you sometimes."

"Will you? Honest?"

"I'll sure try."

"When?"

"Well, I'll probably be back through here next Sunday afternoon."

"I'll look for you."

I wanted to kiss her, but I didn't. I squeezed her hand once and left her standing in the pine grove as I ran to the car. Her mama didn't even stick her head out to yell goodbye. I got into the car. Floyd, smoking a cigarette, looked about half asleep, the smoke running up along his face so that his eyes stayed half closed.

There was only a mile of the dirt road until we ran into the graveled highway State 12.

I said, "What time is it, Floyd?"

"Nine-thirty. Don't worry, Mark. You got a lot of time to get down to Jackson."

It was strange that we had been at that house only an hour, yet it seemed we had spent half the day there.

Floyd yawned, stretching his mouth wide like a big cat, and when he blew the air back out he seemed to shudder and chop his jaws together as though he had a bad taste in his mouth. "Jesus," he said. "Jesus."

"What's wrong, Floyd?"

He smiled slowly and shook his head. "That damned stuff knocks me out this time of day. I don't know why the hell I do it—except I just hate to pass it up. You know what I mean?"

I nodded. "Floyd, Geraldine is fourteen. How—er, how old is her mama?"

"Thirty-two. Sure, sure she's got a few years on me. But when they're older it makes them mellow like good whiskey. Don't ever get the idea that the young stuff is always the best, Mark."

"Oh, I never have said that."

Floyd grinned at me. "The main thing is not to pass any of it up, because what you pass up—the way I see it—is what you're going to miss later."

45

"I suppose so."

The last half mile of the dirt road was the driest stretch, out in the open between two cotton fields. The dust billowed up behind the red Ford as the tires spanked into the yellow dirt. Floyd had to turn left at State 12 and drive about another mile and a half into McCool, but I had to start south. Floyd made his turn and stopped the car. The heavy yellow dust seemed to flow right out to the red gravel of the other road.

"There's not even a damned filling station here," Floyd said. "Ride on with me into McCool and I'll buy you a Coke. It'll wash some of this dust out of your mouth."

"Thanks anyway, Floyd. But I guess I ought to get out here. I might miss somebody heading south while we're driving into town."

"You might but I damned sure doubt it. You know, Mark, if your luck's bad it might be night before you get to Jackson."

"I'm not afraid of the dark. Besides, I'll stand in a lighted place."

"You got the guts, Mark. You'll be okay."

I looked at him a few seconds, about the straightest I ever looked him in the eye. "Floyd, you'd better be careful yourself."

"What?"

"Geraldine's daddy. She says he's mean."

Floyd made a scoffing noise. "That old bast don't bother me."

I was standing outside the car, holding my grip to keep from putting it down where all that red dust was. Floyd stuck his hand out. He was holding a dollar. "Take it," he said. "If you get stuck somewhere later, you can always catch the bus on in."

"I couldn't take it, Floyd. I appreciate it, I really do, but I just hate to borrow money. You see, I already owe you fifty cents really, and I owe—"

Floyd shook his head and stuck the dollar back in his pocket. "Yeah, you owe Mattie the washwoman." He raced the motor a little. "Watch yourself. Be careful."

I smiled at him. "I'll pay you the fifty cents for this ride when I get my job building privies for the WPA."

"Tell you what. I ain't going to pass up any bacon and eggs waiting for that fifty cents. See you, Mark."

He gunned his red car up the road and left a trail of choking red dust, like the Devil with his cloak flying out behind him.

THREE

I MUST have waited an hour before I got another ride. I was so discouraged that I started thinking about turning around and trying to catch a ride back to Wesley. The only thing was that nobody came by going back to Wesley. Even on State 12 most of the traffic was going northeast, some of it nice fast cars that went barreling by like their drivers were trying to outrun that choking red dust that stayed with them no matter how fast they moved. I remembered that some of the bigger boys who did a lot of hitchhiking always said that Friday and Saturday was the good time to go to Jackson because all the salesmen were going back home. Monday wasn't supposed to be any good because the drummers then were leaving their homes in Jackson to start up into the country. But Walt Hunter had told me that morning that exams were about over at Mississippi State, so I might be able to catch somebody coming south from Starkville.

Anyway, after about an hour of that dust I was feeling choked, sort of clogged in the nose. It had been a real dry spring for Mississippi. Only about three weeks ago, there had been a bad dust storm that seemed to blot out the late afternoon sun, but folks said that the dust was caused by Texas and Oklahoma blowing away.

I stood there so long that I got to thinking Floyd might be coming back pretty soon, heading for Wesley with the mail. I would have felt funny standing out there, especially after I had turned down his nice offer to buy me a Coke in McCool. He might even try to get me to go back up and see Geraldine and her mama again. I just didn't feel up to that. And I sure didn't want to go back to Wesley and have all the boys laugh and say that I didn't have the guts to hitchhike to Jackson by myself.

Right when it seemed that I was sure going to be embarrassed by Floyd coming by again I got a ride in an old brown Model-A Ford. The car seemed to be ninety years old, and I knew the driver probably wasn't going very far. But I was glad to get away from that spot. The short leaf pines and oaks and gum trees were mighty pretty, but I almost couldn't see them from the dust stirred up by that traffic headed northeast.

The driver was dressed in farmer's khakis, and he looked about as lean as some of those posts holding the barbed wire along the cornfields. His brown eyes seemed lost in their deep sockets, and his face was almost fire-red from sunburn. But when he took off his hat to scratch his head for a few seconds, he not only didn't have any hair but his brow and the top of his head were almost snow-white. The snow-white line came down just above his eyes, and it made the strangest sight—half of his face red, the top part and his head white, and those deep-set dark pits for eyes. It looked really sort of scary. It seemed to me that he ought to leave his hat off out in the sun for a week or so and let the rest of his head redden up. But then, of course, nobody in his right mind wants the hot summer sun beating down on the top of his head. Anyway, that was his business, not mine.

I said, "How far are you going, sir?"

"To Ethel."

Just like I figured. That was only seven miles, but the way that A-Model was crawling along, it was going to feel more like seventy before we got there.

"Are you saved, boy?"

That's what he really said, but it came so sudden and fast that I didn't understand him. I thought he asked was I sick. I said, "Oh, no sir, I'm fine."

"God save you, boy. No man can be fine with a palsy of the soul. 'Remember now thy Creator in the days of thy youth, while the evil days come not, nor the years draw nigh, when thou shalt say, I have no pleasure in them.' Ecclesiastes twelve-one."

I said, " 'While the sun, or the light, or the moon, or the stars, be not darkened, nor the clouds return after the rain.' Ecclesiastes twelve-two."

"God bless you for a Christian, lad. 'For God shall bring every work into judgment, with every secret thing, whether it be good, or whether it be evil.' Ecclesiastes twelve-fourteeen."

I sure wished he hadn't used that verse. There I sat with my hand and fingers not yet washed, fresh from playing around with that shiny black hair-patch on Geraldine. I had done a dark secret thing, and I wasn't sure that I wouldn't have done more if I'd stayed there longer.

I said, "Thank you, sir. God bless you too." And then, the way I am, I couldn't stop myself. I had to keep on quoting. " 'Vanity of vanities, saith the preacher; all is vanity.' Ecclesiastes twelve-eight."

He turned his eyes from the road and stared at me so long that I got a little worried. Even if the car wasn't going very fast, we could have ended up in the ditch if he didn't watch that gravel.

When he finally spoke, his voice sounded like he was trembling inside. "Art thou John come out from the wilderness, lad?"

I sort of smiled. "No sir. I'm just Mark Torrance come out from Wesley Academy."

He nodded, his brown eyes burning from their deep sockets. "Aye, sure, sure. I'm Lance Godbold, lad."

"It's sure a pleasure to know you, sir. I didn't know you lived around here. I believe Mother Joan said it was up in Columbus."

"I've lived there. And Kosciusko. And all around. Right now I'm staying down the road a ways. No man is permanent in this world. 'The foxes have holes, and the birds of the air have nests, but the Son of man hath not where to lay his head.' Matthew eight-twenty."

I had heard Mother Joan speak about Lance Godbold several times, about how next to Gypsy Smith and Howard Williams about the best two Christian evangelists in the South were John Gabriel and Lance Godbold. Mr. Godbold had been a scholar in England for a time, but he was supposed to have seen the light and come back to his native soil to spread God's word. Looking at him now, I was proud to be riding with him, but I couldn't quite figure the situation out. I mean, John Gabriel had come to Wesley with a house-on-wheels that would have matched the best suite of rooms in the Heidelberg Hotel in Jackson. And Howard Williams during a seven-day revival in which he spoke twice a day had never worn the same suit twice. Walt Hunter, about the fanciest dresser up at the Square, said that shoes like Mr. Williams wore, black suede and patent leather, cost about twenty dollars a pair. But this Lance Godbold sure looked to be a very poor man.

Suddenly again, but slowly, he said, " 'Seek ye the Lord while he may be found . . .' "

He just left the verse hanging in mid-air like that, so I finished it, " 'Call ye upon him while he is near.' "

He nodded, but didn't look at me. " 'Blessed are the pure in heart: for they shall see God.' "

I said, " 'Blessed are the peacemakers: for they shall be called the children of God.' "

We zipped through the rest of the Beatitudes, even going back to quote the ones at the beginning too. We started throwing verses like wild-fire, like we were having a reciting contest for a big prize. Then Mr. Godbold went back and would say the first half of a verse, and I would come along and finish it up. He never even looked my way when he thundered out the first part of the verses; he just seemed satisfied that I was going to be able to finish them all right.

I knew all these verses because I was a good Christian who

actively attended Mother Joan's prayer band up at Wesley. Out of the seventy or so boys at the Square, only about five of us attended regularly. Mother Joan was the mother of a former president of Wesley Academy. After he was killed when a gravel pit bank caved in one day while he was digging, they named one of the buildings after him—probably the one they were getting the sand and gravel for that day. And they kept his wife on as a teacher of Bible classes. Mrs. Mahan was a beautiful blonde-haired woman with the clearest, brightest blue eyes I ever saw. Her skin was always soft and smooth, even though there were a few little lines around the eyes. I didn't really know how long her husband had been dead, but I would have guessed five or six years. It had been a few years, I know, because the Mahan son, who was about eleven, told me one day that he could hardly remember his father. And Mrs. Mahan had reached the point she allowed 'Fessor King to escort her around a little bit. A few times this spring they had driven to Ackerman or Kosciusko to shop on Saturdays.

Anyway, Mother Joan was the mother-in-law of Mrs. Mahan. They lived together with the eleven-year-old boy in a kind of three-room apartment deal up at the Square. Actually the way the Square was, sort of block U-shaped, they lived at the center of the U's bottom, where a large front porch like an old mansion had been built. The rest of the Square was one-storied, but there at the bottom was a second story with two rooms. I think it was a nice thing to have those fine ladies up there in the boys' dormitory that way. 'Fessor King had his own room over at a corner of the U. He kept down any really rough stuff, but he couldn't be there all the time. Just knowing that Mother Joan might be upstairs looking from one of her windows was enough to keep some of the more unruly guys decent. Even at that, I'll bet Mother Joan and Mrs. Mahan saw plenty of things they weren't supposed to, things that would embarrass them to have to discuss. I mean, for example, that some people you just can't civilize—like J. D. Stuckey, who goes round the Square about half-naked. Plenty of the boys sometimes skip from room to room like that, but I've seen J.D., just on a foolish bet, after taking off a sweaty football uniform, run naked across the middle of the Square, almost fifty yards, to get to the shower room. J.D. didn't seem to care who saw him that way. His first name was John, and although everyone usually just called him J.D., he was always saying that he wanted to be called "Long John."

Mother Joan was the smallest little lady you could ever hope to see. I wouldn't know how old she was, but her skin was as white and crinkly as tissue paper. She was always dressed in black dresses and shawls so that her body seemed to have no shape at all. She always looked like a short black cylinder with snow-white hair whenever you'd see her moving along the sidewalk—which wasn't very often, because she just didn't get out too much. I think she spent most of her time in the little room where her prayer band met every week night at six-thirty, a half hour before study hall. The room was very small, it had a pump organ, a lot of religious stuff on the walls—and for some reason it always smelled like the sickish sweet flowers in a funeral parlor. Funny, the only funeral I've attended—my little cousin who died two summers ago—the main thing I remembered was the sick-sweet flower smell. They didn't let me look into the casket.

Of the five boys in the prayer band one was naturally the Mahan boy I've mentioned. Another was Richard Livingstone, a sixteen-year-old who was about the most mournful-faced Christian I've ever seen. Some of the boys said the reason he went around so long-faced was that his folks had named him Richard instead of David. The great African missionary was his hero, and Richard said he was going to follow his hero's footsteps in Africa. Richard went around the Square ringing the prayer band bell each night, and it was sinful what some of those older boys would say to him by way of insults. The third boy was Allison McGee. Why he attended prayer band I don't really know. He was very bright, about the toughest competition I had in making grades at school. And he was always working with inventions and stuff, always thinking about some project. He had even been teaching himself to play the organ, practicing there in the prayer band room. Well, I don't say Allison was a hypocrite or anything like that, and we never discussed it, but he would go to prayer band at six-thirty, sing "Jesus Wants Me for a Sunbeam" or "Let the Lower Lights Be Burning," lead us in prayer if it was his turn, and then within the same hour be sending J. D. Stuckey notes in study hall asking to take a look at J.D.'s nasty pictures. Allison said it didn't hurt him any to go to prayer band, and even if he was a little hypocritical, at least he didn't sneer and say nasty things to Richard when he was ringing the bell. Allison said he wouldn't hurt Mother Joan's feelings for a million dollars. But that was the prayer band—just the three boys I've mentioned, plus me and Carl. Carl had been skipping pretty often lately too. He said he was getting a little stale from all the doses of religion, that twice a day was enough and after supper was just too much. But he didn't stay away too often, because he knew Mother Joan's feelings would be hurt.

The result of all these Bible classes and Sunday school and prayer band was that I knew a great deal of Scripture. I had read the whole Bible, even though I sped through a lot of the "begat" chapters in the Old Testament. I not only read the Scripture, but I pondered it too. I was a little disturbed by the notion that unless a man became a Christian he was doomed to everlasting hellfire. This worried me because, apart from all the Chinese, Africans, and other known heathens, I had to face the fact that I wasn't even sure about my own father and mother and other relatives. Once I asked Mrs. Mahan in Bible class about all those heathen Chinese that were going to Hell. She said I was being enlightened and it was my responsibility, and that of every other Christian, to teach those heathens the true religion before it was too late. It was quite a challenge all right, because even if you got to some of them there would be plenty more you couldn't help but miss. And there must be millions of heathens who died before I was ever born to help them. It just didn't seem right that they had to burn just because they weren't born to the advantages of a Christian place like Wesley. I mentioned this to Mrs. Mahan, but she said religion was like eating fish—just chew the meaty parts and leave the bones alone. Then she repeated that it was my duty to go out and convert the heathens. I nodded my head, but actually I was more worried about getting to my own father first. He's fifty-eight years old, a kind of rough-and-tumble bricklayer who has been known to drink pretty heavy on paydays but who, when the work is available, is always out there bright and early on Monday mornings. I do wish I could make certain he was saved.

Pretty soon Lance Godbold quit throwing verses at me. I still had a few in reserve, but he seemed to play out on the idea. He kept driving, staring at the road, the red-skinned lower jaw rippling a muscle when he clamped his teeth together. Up ahead I saw a little dirt road off to the left, and he started slowing the Model-A down. We had been riding twenty minutes or so, so I figured the little town of Ethel was just over the hill. I didn't recognize anything, because I had only been over that way once, when Daddy and Mama brought Carl and me to Wesley from Jackson last fall. When we'd hit this section back then, it was raining so hard and the car was throwing so much mud around I wouldn't have been able to remember anything except what the headlights showed, rain hitting the windshield, the car heading into what looked like a deep orange molasses puddle. The tires had slopped through that mud like a mortar man's hoe churning up the sand, water, and cement on one of Daddy's jobs.

Mr. Godbold stopped the car after he turned into the road. When I started to get out, he put his hand on my arm.

"Wait, Mark, are you in a hurry?"

"No sir, I just want to get down to Jackson before dark."

"I need your help, boy. The Lord has sent you for a sign."

Well, I didn't know if the Lord had that in mind or not, but I did know why the Reverend Ingram had sent me. I didn't know what to say to Mr. Godbold. I just looked at him.

"Will you come with me for just a short time, lad? I want you to pray with me."

I said, "Why don't we pray right here?"

"No, come along with me to my house. About a hundred yards down the road. Then you'll see what we're praying for."

I looked back up State 12 from where we'd come. A few cars had passed us while the old Model-A was churning along, but I didn't see any dust being stirred back that way now.

He said, "You won't need to stay long, lad. And there's a chance you might get a ride to Kosciusko."

"All right. That would be fine."

Like he said, the place was only a little ways off State 12. We went up the dirt road and turned off into a little pine-filled hollow. A few of the bigger trees had been cleared off a long time ago, because a lot of stumps were still around, some of which had been a chopped at pretty badly by someone looking for veins of rich pine to use for kindling. In the middle of the hollow was a small unpainted shack, the wood turned a kind of soggy gray from the weather, the whole thing on stilts a couple of feet off the ground. I didn't see any stock around—no barn, no garden, and certainly no fields planted with cotton, corn, or cane.

A V-8 Ford was parked by the house—a new Ford about like Floyd's except that it was black instead of red. But like Floyd's, even though it was new it was starting to look pretty beat up. These country roads take a lot out of a car in a short time, Willie Jefferson told me one day. Willie was fullback on our team last fall. He weighs about two-forty and has an eighteen-inch neck. Mississippi State grabbed him in a hurry to play for them next fall. Unlike a lot of the Wesley football players, Willie is no dummy. He knows a lot about cars.

"Come along, Mark," Mrs. Godbold said.

I looked at my suitcase for a second and then decided that it was certainly in no danger of being stolen out there, especially in front of the evangelist Lance Godbold's house. Just as I was starting up the plank steps to the porch, a big solid black dog stretched out from the shadows under the house. He was some kind of mongrel mixture with low-hanging jaws. Right away he took a sniff of me. The dog seemed as big as I was—which, of course, he really wasn't. But he was big enough he could have pulled my arm off just for light exercise.

"Down, Simon," Mr. Godbold said. "Simon's a good dog, but he gets angry too easily. Just pat him on the head."

I gave Simon the fastest pat ever seen by dog or man, then followed Mr. Godbold into the house. Over in one corner of the house—which was really this big one-room shack, to be perfectly honest—someone was lying on a thin mattress on the floor. A man in dark trousers and white shirt with green suspenders was kneeling beside the bed. The man glanced around at us for a second, but then turned back to the person on the mattress.

The big room was sure stripped down, almost as bare-looking as something Daniel Boone might have stayed in. There was a little wood-burning stove about the size of the ones we hooked up in our rooms during the winter at Wesley, a wooden icebox with the white paint peeling off, a table and three chairs, and some kind of chest with a mirror hanging in front of it. I didn't see anything that looked like a closet, but some long sticks rigged caty-cornered to the walls held some clothes on hangers. A couple of trunks were over against the other wall.

The man kneeling by the bed stood up and turned to us. He was about the age of Mr. Godbold, maybe younger, but he might have just seemed younger because he had hair.

The man said, "She's better, Lance. She's sleeping right now."

"Aye, she needs the rest."

"I'm glad you're back. I have to be going."

Mr. Godbold grabbed the man's hand and shook it. "I appreciate what you've done, Tom. How's the child?"

The man looked at Mr. Godbold and shook his head very slowly from one side to the other.

Mr. Godbold said, "No better? No better at all?"

I could see the black case down by the mattress, almost covered by the top sheet that was partly slid off the mattress. The doctor looked at Mr. Godbold for a few seconds, then shook his head and kind of gritted his teeth. He said, "Goddamit, Lance, I told you what it's going to take to save the baby!"

Mr Godbold's face got red at the top half too. But it was sort of like someone had opened a gate and let the red flood waters rush to the top of his head. He said, "God forgive you, Tom. If you've no respect for me, at least have some for my wife and child and this young boy here."

The doctor nodded his head slowly in a kind of tired disgust. His face had long lines working out from the eyes, lines that seemed to dig into his cheeks like rivers cutting through hills. His dark beard was heavy and his eyes red.

The doctor said, "I'm sorry, Lance. I'm a little short this morning, a little edgy. About the only place I run into a situation like this is at a nigger shanty someplace. But even they have sense enough to let their babes go to the hospital."

Mr. Godbold said, "We need no hospital. No child of mine will go to a charity ward."

"All right! Damn the charity ward. Get money when you preach! Borrow some from me. Hell, I'll give you money."

"If you have money to give, Tom, then give it freely. But not to me. The poor, the hungry are always with us. Inasmuch as ye have done it unto one of the least of these my brethren, ye have done it unto me."

The doctor shrugged his shoulders. He reached into his shirt pocket and pulled out a pack of Camel cigarettes.

Mr. Godbold said, "I've brought a boy to pray, Tom."

"You have, huh? Well, it's too bad you couldn't bring a nurse with an oxygen tent."

Mr. Godbold shook his head slowly. "We don't need that. God is the great physician."

The doctor put the cigarette in his mouth. "Well, I'm not God and neither are you—no matter what you may think."

Mr. Godbold said, "Will you pray with us, Tom?"

The doctor shook his head. "I'd rather smoke."

"But," Mr. Godbold said, "maybe you'll at least wait and give this boy a ride to Kosciusko with you. He'll be leaving as soon as we finish praying."

Those bloodshot eyes looked at me. Then the doctor nodded. "I'll wait for him out on the porch. But don't let the prayer last longer than my cigarette."

The doctor walked out to the porch. I still hadn't seen any baby. Mr. Godbold put his hands on my shoulders and guided me around to the other side of the mattress. A couple of flies were buzzing around, and he waved his hand to shoo them away. Then he turned back the cover that was almost hiding the woman's face. She was a pale, dark-haired woman with the baby under her right arm sleeping against her bosom. That pale woman looked tired all right, but what really surprised me was the baby. I hadn't seen too many young babies, certainly not many fresh-born ones, but this had to be the smallest baby in the state of Mississippi. I remember when those little Dionne girls were born in Canada a couple of years ago that the five of them altogether only weighed about fourteen pounds. This one wasn't as small as any of them, but he was red and shrunken, like a tiny celluloid doll, with perfect little fingers and toes but with arms and legs that didn't look any bigger than a fountain pen. Its eyes were closed, and it puffed and wheezed its breath like some kind of newborn baby bird that had fallen from its nest to the ground. A fly zoomed down while Mr. Godbold held the cover back. I shooed the fly away.

Mr. Godbold pulled the cover back up and put his hand on my shoulder again. "We'll pray, lad."

"Yes sir."

The sunlight was streaming through the one window, hitting the sleeping woman full in the face, but she didn't turn or stir.

We kneeled down beside the mattress.

Mr. Godbold said, "We'll pray silently for a minute or so,

Mark. Then I'll pray aloud and ask you to finish with a little prayer after me."

"Yes sir."

My knees were hard against the pine floor, and I could smell what was left on the stove of a pot of early morning coffee. I tried to blot all this out of my mind so I could come into God's presence. I bowed my head and closed my eyes, and I kept still like that even though one of the flies started buzzing over my ear.

My eyes shut tight like that, I really noticed the little baby's breathing, like the rasp of a small file. I prayed hard, silently, because I knew when I started praying out loud in a few minutes it was going to sound artificial and maybe insincere. When you pray and someone is hearing you—I mean, besides God— then you always keep watching the way you put your sentences together. But right now it was just God and me. "Dear God, please help your fine servant, thy minister Mr. Godbold. About all he seems to have in this old shack is a lot of faith in You. This little baby just doesn't seem to have any chance at all, that doctor said, but You can save this little child even if there isn't any oxygen tent. Your own Son walked on the water and that's much harder than just putting a little more air into this baby's lungs. Lord, he that believeth in You shall never die, but this little baby hasn't lived long enough to know whether—"

Well, that really did it! Right when I was going good, Satan had stepped into my prayer and got me to wondering whether this little baby would go to Heaven if it died. Because Mrs. Mahan had said that little babies, just like the older heathens, would go one place or the other. If it seems bad to think of helpless heathens in Hell, just imagine a nice fat little baby that never had any chance of its own to decide about God lying down under, frying in the vats of Hell. A person might just figure in a case like this that if the baby of evangelist Lance Godbold can't get to Heaven then no baby can, but it's a problem that no one really knows the answer to.

I was about to pray silently again, but just then Mr. Godbold came on strong, praying out loud. "Almighty Father, ruler of heaven and earth, Thou has promised that where two or three are gathered together in Thy name that there art Thou in the midst of them . . ."

I noticed, as he kept praying, that he used some fine phrases that would have made Reverend Ingram a little envious. Not that Mr. Ingram didn't have some fine language too, but mostly his words stood out only when he was threatening sinners with damnation or talking about how unworthy the congregation was. Bob Durham, an admittedly infidel person, once said that the trouble with Mr. Ingram was that you couldn't always tell whether he was praying to God or giving Him orders. But Mr. Godbold prayed thankfully, even in his time of trouble.

He said, "O Lord, Thou knowest what I will make of this child if Thou keep life in his veins. Thou knowest too how much the world needs such a child. Thy mercies upon us then, O Lord."

He nudged me.

I said, "The Lord is my refuge and strength, a very present help in time of trouble. Dear God, Thy Son said to suffer the little children to come unto Him, but please don't take this one yet—unless You just absolutely have to have him now. Let him stay and be a joy to his father and mother. But Thy will be done. Amen."

Just as I finished the prayer, I brought up a quarter from my pocket, and while I knew Mr. Godbold's eyes were still closed, I slipped the quarter right beneath the little corner of sheet that was on the floor. Later, when the sheet was moved, he would find it.

As we got to our feet, he clasped my right hand in both of his. "Bless you, Mark. God bless you, boy."

"I hope your baby will get well, sir."

"The child shall live. Faith shall make him live."

The doctor came walking back in very quickly. He took one more look at the mother and picked up his little black bag.

He looked at me. "Let's be going, son."

Mr. Godbold said, "Thank you again, Tom, for all you've done."

The doctor snorted, "Done what? Given you a lot of advice you won't take. Well, do what you can. One thing might help—fix that screen, keep some of these damned flies out of here."

"I'll do that this very hour, Tom."

I followed the doctor down the front planks. The black dog came out and sniffed us again. Mr. Godbold said, "Down, Simon."

I hurried to take my bag from the A-Model and catch up with the doctor. Just as we got to the doctor's car, Mr. Godbold called out, "Thanks again, Tom. I'll be praying for you."

The doctor seemed to grind his jaws together and let out a fast hissing sound that ended in a whisper, "Jesus Christ." Then he looked toward the house and called back, "I'll check back again tonight."

Mr. Godbold waved, I waved back, and the doctor headed the car out to the road. After we got on State 12, he started rolling pretty fast into Kosciusko, a distance of about eight miles. He didn't say anything at first—just drove as though he was deadly intent on getting there in a hurry. The new gravel was loose, and sometimes the car swerved as the tires ran uneasy into it. But the doctor held her to the road, not seeming to mind the way the big rocks whammed up under the fenders.

He didn't say a word till we were almost into Kosciusko. Then all at once he laughed aloud but as though it were to himself, and he glanced at me. "Well, son, you probably think I'm a real bastard, don't you?"

"Sir?"

"I said you think I'm a big bastard, don't you?"

"Well, I don't—I mean, why should I think that?"

He shook his head again. Then he asked about me, how old I was, where I was going—you know, all that. When I said I was thirteen, he seemed surprised to know that I was out on the road by myself. But then he said, "You'll get home all right.

You look like a sensible boy—a boy with common sense that can't be fooled. How much money do you have?"

When I told him thirty cents, he said, "Don't tell me those fine Christians at Wesley put you on the damned highway with thirty cents in your pocket!"

"Well, no sir. I had fifty-five when I left, but I left a quarter back in Mr. Godbold's house, back by the baby. He might could use it to buy milk or something."

He laughed and hissed again, his body shaking and jerking. When he finally stopped that, he looked at me. "I'm not laughing at you, boy. I think you did a nice thing. But that's about the way things run for Lance—squeezing a kid like you for half of what you got."

"He didn't squeeze me for anything. When he finds that quarter he probably won't even know where it came from."

"Oh, he'll know all right. And he'll drop down on his knees and thank that God of his for making you such a fine boy and then he'll keep on praying about bringing the whole world back to the kingdom of Heaven. A dying baby on his hands, and he'll spend half the day wallowing on his knees praying to something he can't see—while the flies buzz round that baby's head."

"He said he was going to fix the screen."

"Christ was supposed to be a good carpenter. Lance ain't."

"Do you really think the baby will die, sir?"

"There's no way it can live another two days."

"We prayed—"

"Damn it, boy, prayer won't clear snot and fluid out of the lungs. That baby's three months early."

"I can see why Mr. Godbold wouldn't want to take charity or anything like that. But it is hard to see why he won't take the baby to some hospital."

The doctor snorted again. "Wants to test his faith, prove his God the hard way. Why, he might's well take a goddam water moccasin and wrap it around his neck like some of these other religious nuts. Faith, hell! This goddam car don't run on faith, boy. It takes gas! He's made money, Lance has—a helluva lot of money. But as fast as some rednecks give to him, he gives it back to others. Won't keep a goddam penny for himself."

I said, "The Lord Jesus did that too."

"Well, the Lord Jesus didn't marry and try to have a child born to his wife in a fly-specked shack."

I was wondering about it, so finally I asked, "Doesn't Mr. Godbold's wife mind the way they live?"

"Oh, he won't be in that place there long. After the baby dies he'll be on his way again. They'll live in some places better, but for damned sure a lot worse too. It's a pity, but now I think the wife is about as nutty as Lance is."

Up ahead I saw the square with the courthouse in the center. The doctor pulled up and turned left at the first stop light on the square.

He pointed down the other street. "State 12 runs on that way. Good luck, son."

I got my grip from the car, then stuck my hand back in. He smiled at me and shook my hand. I said, "In spite of all you said, I still think you're a very good man, doctor. You did go out of your way to help Mrs. Godbold and her baby. It's real fine of you."

He shook his head. "Thanks, son, but that won't put any stars in my crown. Lance is my brother."

He shook his head again. I backed off as the car moved on down the street.

FOUR

AFTER THE doctor let me out, it was almost eleven-thirty by the courthouse clock. As I walked past the square, moving on down so I could catch the traffic at the outskirts of town, I decided that I ought to get something to eat. I had had some cornflakes and five biscuits with syrup that morning, but being on the road sure burns a man's food in a hurry. I went into a little greasy-spoon sort of cafe, one that—no matter how it looked—served a good lunch of meat loaf, potatoes, and turnip greens for a quarter. I hated to spend that much, because I could have bought a Mr. Goodbar and a glass of milk for just a dime. But since there was no telling what time I'd finally get down to Jackson I thought I needed a good nourishing meal. I had only a nickel left when I finished paying for the meal, but I figured if I got stuck somewhere I could use that for a Goodbar or a Baby Ruth and that would last me into the night.

I picked up a map from a Gulf service station. From Kosciusko to Durant was twenty miles. State 12, running in a long twisting blue line southwest from Alabama, really sort of went straight west, maybe even a little north, in that stretch to Durant from Kosciusko. It looked like the last gravel stretch I would have. I would run into US 51 at Durant, a concrete highway going all the way down to New Orleans. I was so tired of breathing that red gravel dust that I kept thinking about that white concrete of 51 like it was some kind of magic carpet that would just roll me down to Jackson in a matter of five minutes or so.

I followed the street out a ways until finally down the hill I could see only one more block of pavement before the gravel road started again. Down the road, maybe a hundred yards or so, two men were standing. They must have been college boys going home from Mississippi State because I could make out the big red M on one of the suitcases facing the traffic. I thought about walking down and talking to them and maybe telling them that State was going to get a great football prospect from Wesley in the fall by name of Willie Jefferson. But I decided that three of us standing together might make it tougher to catch a ride. So I turned and faced the traffic and concentrated on smiling at all the drivers of the cars coming toward me. I was trying to let them know that I was a nice clean-cut boy who wouldn't hop in their cars and try to cut their throats or something. I felt kind of foolish, grinning at those drivers like a possum, but I figured I ought to do what I could to help myself.

There seemed to be a good bit of traffic stirring there at the noon hour, but most of it was just local stuff—men shifting round from the cotton gins and sawmills at the edge of town. Still, I couldn't know for sure where all those cars were going. I kept smiling.

"Where you heading, kid?"

I turned around, very surprised. I hadn't been looking back down the road for a couple of minutes. One of the college boys had come up to talk to me.

I said, "Hi. I'm going to Jackson."

"You got a smoke?"

"What? Oh, no, I don't smoke. I'm sorry."

He was a very tall guy, probably twenty or so, pretty well-dressed. His face had a few little pocks in it, and when he talked he kept rubbing a large mole on his chin.

He asked where I was from. When I told him Wesley Academy, he nodded his head. "I figured you for a schoolboy.

That's a nice-looking grip you got there."

"Thanks, but it's not really mine. It's my daddy's. It sure is a fine grip. The inside has a nice smell—you know, sort of leathery—and all red and smooth."

"Look, kid, me and my partner down there been thinking about you."

"Oh, you have?"

"Yeah. And we decided we don't like it a goddamned bit you walking out and parking your ass up here in front of us."

My face turned red. "Gosh, I didn't even think about that."

"You start thinking, baby. First come, first served—that's the rule of the road."

I nodded. "Well, sure. That's the way it ought to be."

I was really embarrassed that I had been too ignorant not to know such an important rule. I hated for this college boy to think I had never hitchhiked before. I picked up my grip and followed him down the road, my feet slapping up dust as we hit the gravel again. The other college guy was very short. His dark hair was slicked down flat on his head. As we came up to him, I nodded and kept on walking.

The short one said, "Sorry, kid, but we got to have first crack."

I said, "Sure. It's okay."

The tall one said, "He's a schoolboy. Going home from Wesley Academy."

The short one said, "Boys go to Wesley, men go to Mississippi State, and pigs go to Ole Miss."

They laughed, the short one especially, like he really appreciated his own joke. I smiled and kept on walking.

The short one called after me, "Say, buddy, you got a cigarette?"

The other one said, "Naw, I already asked him. The kids at Wesley don't smoke."

"Hey, that's right." The short one looked at me. "You know that poem, don't you, kid?

> *"Rooty-toot-toot, rooty-toot-toot,*
> *We're the boys from the Institute.*
> *We don't smoke and we don't chew,*
> *And we don't go with the gals that screw."*

I said, "Yeah, I know that poem."

I went on down about a hundred yards beyond them. The more I walked through that dusty gravel with that sun popping smack down on my head, the more I started getting mad. Of course, I really had nothing to get mad about. I *had* violated a rule of the road. But the more I thought about it, the more I decided I didn't like the way they'd talked to me—especially that tall one when he had first walked up. Not that I could do anything about it.

Pretty soon a tremendous-sized Negro appeared up at about the same place where I had been standing the first time. He waited there for a minute or two, then I could see the tall college boy waving his arm and yelling something. The big Negro started walking. When he passed the two college boys, I could see they were saying something to him, but he just kept walking on. The closer he came, the more he reminded me of Big Boy, who lived outside of Wesley.

Big Boy is one of the most tremendous Negro giants I've seen, and I've seen some big ones. He stands six-eight and weighs about two-ninety, and his biceps are the size of small pumpkins. Big Boy became a friend of mine just a month or so ago back in the spring when we were playing baseball. One Saturday afternoon Big Boy and another Negro had been hanging around the ball field where some of us had chosen sides. Two of the white boys had to leave pretty early, so we had let the Negroes play. I was catching for one team. My daddy bought me a catcher's mitt when I was about nine years old, and I had been catching ever since. For a kid my age I could handle pitchers pretty well. No matter how hot they threw I would catch the ball just right, making it smack loud into the mitt. The older boys liked to pitch to me because I kept a steady target, and the way I could make that ball pop it always made them think they were really burning the ball in—whether they were or not.

Anyway, that afternoon our pitcher tired out in three innings, and even though the other side complained that it wasn't fair we let Big Boy pitch for us. Well, as I said, I've caught a few hot pitchers. Down in Jackson, in fact, I used to meet the visiting teams of the East Dixie League as they walked from the hotel to their bus, and I would persuade the manager to let me be batboy for them. That way I not only got in the game free—which didn't matter too much, since I could have jumped the fence with the rest of the kids—but I also got cracked bats and now and then a ball from the manager, especially if his team had beaten Jackson that night. Sometimes before the game, I would go out by the bleachers and warm up some of the pitchers. Mostly, though, it was outfielders who would clown around while they played catch with me. They thought it was funny that small as I was I could still catch their fast balls or sharp-breaking curves. That's what I like about baseball. You don't have to be the size of a lunk-headed ox in order to play. I mean, more size would certainly give me more hitting power and maybe help strengthen my throwing arm, but I doubt if I'll ever be able to catch that ball any better than I can right now.

Well, that afternoon Big Boy had really burned and curved that ball in there. He was so hot that I sometimes felt the force of the ball would knock me back off my haunches when I caught it. Big Boy struck out eight of the ten batters that faced him. Later I felt very proud when he said, "Mister Mark, you gonna be the best baseball catcher ever lived." I took such talk with a grain of salt, but it was still nice hearing that from a man that could have probably been a big leaguer himself if they had let Negroes play up there. And after that day, I was always one of the first to be chosen when the olders boys started picking sides. Just about anybody can run around the outfield chasing flies, but it takes a sharp catcher to keep a team going.

This Negro walking up toward me looked exactly like Big Boy—maybe not quite as big. There was a grin on his face.

I said, "They sent you down the road too, huh?"

He grinned. "Not exactly, young boss. I thought I might's well walk on down so's they wouldn't get uncheerful."

It was pretty ridiculous when you think about it. Two simpleton college boys that this Negro, as tough as Samson when he crashed the temple down on the Philistines, could have cracked like two pecans! And yet he had to be careful not to make them mad.

I said, "Why don't you wait and hitchhike with me right here?"

He grinned again and shook his head. "Naw sir, you know I can't do that. I don't be going far nohow. Maybe three miles down the road. Somebody I know will come long pretty soon and pick me up."

I looked back up the road. A car had stopped for the college boys. When it started moving again, I watched it close, trying to decide whether it was slowing to pick me up. It seemed to be at first, but then it picked up speed and shot on past me, stirring up the dust. The short one waved at me from the front seat.

The traffic died down. The few cars that did go by, most of the drivers would signal to let me know that they were turning off just down the road. I remembered that I hadn't practiced my declamation for a couple of hours. Since I was all by myself, I went back to that tough section of the speech—the one I had tried to practice when I was with Geraldine. I said, "Don't you see what I mean? Don't you see what I am driving at? Ladies and gentlemen, what are we to do with this wretched, desperate brother of ours—who will not obey us though we lock him behind bars of iron? Though we whip him with a cat-o'-nine-tails, and though we finally take that rebellious life on the gallows, he will die with a snarl on his lips and a curse in his heart!"

But I couldn't keep my mind on the declamation. I thought about the little Godbold child for a few minutes, and then, like it was the strangest dream I ever had, I remembered Geraldine under the pine trees with that little patch of black hair. I knew that I had been at the Godbold place and prayed for that baby. I could remember the smell of the old shack and the zooming of the flies and the hardness of the floor on my knees when I prayed. But looking back in my mind, I seemed to be watching someone else put his fingers into that black hair-patch. I felt uneasy that I could get that little baby and the praying and the white skin and hair-patch all mixed together like that.

I thought about the pledge I had made at John Gabriel's revival no more than a month ago. John Gabriel had held two special sessions—one for women and one for men. Well, I don't know what he told the ladies, but he was sure at his best when he talked to the men. He talked about lust, fornication, and adultery in a way I had never hoped to hear a respectable man talk. I was really pretty shocked when he told about the consequences of social diseases. I had never heard anyone—except maybe the likes of Bob Durham or J. D. Stuckey—come right out and talk about gonorrhea and syphilis the way John Gabriel did. A person could see that even the slightest contact with evil women might just cause the person to end up with that whole private part of his body dropping off like a loose fender from a worn-out T-model Ford. Well, all that didn't worry me too much personally, since I didn't plan to ever in my life have any contact with any known evil women. What worried me was the ones I didn't *know* as evil. Take that good-looking Geraldine for example. She looked as healthy and sweet as a ripe ear of boiled yellow corn with salt and butter running all over it. Why, I couldn't have touched a known prostitute on the hair-patch any more than I could have taken a drink of whiskey. But I hadn't felt that way about Geraldine. John Gabriel quoted Scripture to the effect that a man who even thinks about getting carnal knowledge of a woman has already sinned in his own heart. It seems to me this does make a tough situation for a man. Shun lustful thoughts, the evangelist said, shun them like the plague! But it sure is tough. I had made a pledge to live the clean life no more than a month ago, and here I had already had my fingers in a hair-patch and thought evil in my heart.

The sun was beating down, and my own thoughts sure weren't helping me bear that dust and heat. Everything was bright and heat-wavy, and I kept wishing I was back sitting on a bunk, leaning against one of those cool plaster walls in our room at Wesley. I always get sleepy for a while in the afternoon, no matter how much rest I might have had the night before. Especially after the noon meal I think a short nap is the finest thing in the world.

Then down the hill I saw a new green DeSoto coming. I knew right away that I was going to get a ride, because it was almost as though the driver saw me the minute he topped the hill and decided right then to pick me up. The green DeSoto was so brightly polished that not even the dust seemed to be staying on it. When I put my grip on the back floor and got in the front seat I could smell that new car odor, like it had just come out of a package.

I said, "Are you going all the way to Durant, sir?"

"I am. Is that where you're going?"

"Well, I get on 51 at Durant and go on down to Jackson."

"That's marvelous," he said, sort of grabbing my arm and squeezing it. "You've had wonderful luck. I'm going to Jackson myself."

I smiled at him. "You don't mind if I ride all the way there with you?"

"I wouldn't think of having you do anything else!"

At that I just relaxed all over. It would really be something to tell the guys at Wesley that right when I was getting a little worried and tired I had caught a ride seventy miles long. If we didn't run into too much bad road, we would be down there by three o'clock at least.

I had noticed a couple of briefcases in the back, very expensive-looking and new. I felt proud that Daddy's grip was nothing to be ashamed of, even if it was getting a little dusty. It still looked good alongside that expensive-looking stuff. I could tell right away that this man was a quality person. He was lean-looking and had black wavy hair, and his face had a red quality without being sunburned. He smelled of sweet after-shave, the kind of stuff that the guys at Wesley called "foo-foo" lotion. His suit, a kind of light-summer-gray, was the kind you'd see advertised in *Esquire*. This man was over thirty, but he was the kind of older person who wore stylish clothes well.

He said, "I'm Clifton Sharm, young man."

"I'm Mark Torrance."

"Pleased to know you, Mark." He kept driving with his left hand, but stuck the other one over and we shook. His hand was a little sticky. After I pulled mine back I waited a second or two and then so he wouldn't notice and be offended I sort of rubbed my palm slowly on the side of my trousers.

He offered me a cigarette, and when I said I didn't smoke he told me that was a wonderful thing, that he hated to see younger men become slaves to tobacco. He lit his own cigarette and puffed it very rapidly. He'd hold the cigarette between his fingers and talk, then he'd take a drag off it so fast the cigarette hardly seemed to touch his lips before he pulled it away. He puffed in and out very rapidly, reminding me of some movie Indian up on a hill sending smoke signals so the tribe could ambush the U.S. Cavalry.

"Stay away from tobacco, Mark," he said, while he puffed. "You may get tobacco heart, and it looks to me as though you're going to be a fine athlete. Why, I'll bet you're already playing some splendid football."

"Not really. It might surprise you to know that I weigh only a hundred-ten. Because I'm kind of loose-built, people think I weigh more—but I really don't. I'm just thirteen years old."

He made a face as if he couldn't believe I was so young. "Oh, you'll gain weight very quickly from now on. One day you'll be as fat as I am."

"You're not fat, Mr. Sharm."

"Please, please, Mark. All my friends call me Clif. And I think you're right. I'm really not fat yet. Heaven knows I dread to get that way, but for a while at least I still have my figure. Do tell me about yourself, Mark."

There was no way I could sit there and just start blabbing about myself. So about all I said was that I had a week off from Wesley and was going home to see my folks.

He puckered his lips and said, "Wesley Academy, Wesley Academy—heavens, isn't that the Holy Roller place?"

"No sir, there's nothing Holy Roller about it. They just teach old-fashioned Presbyterian religion."

"Oh, I meant no offense, Mark. Goodness, let's get away from that complicated subject. Do they feed you well at Wesley?"

I told him it probably wasn't the greatest place in the world for food, but that everybody seemed healthy. I told him breakfast was oatmeal or Cream of Wheat in the winter and corn flakes or All-Bran in the spring—along with biscuit and molasses no matter what time of year it was. For supper we also had biscuits with rice or grits and gravy, plus some kind of meat every other day, stuff like a piece of tripe or ham. I said, "And last fall when they slaughtered hogs we really had good suppers for about three weeks—country style sausage every night to go with the grits or rice."

"Mark, it doesn't really sound to me as though you're going to get fat anytime soon."

I felt like some kind of traitor to Wesley for having talked that way. "But the noon meal is always a fine one. Plenty of vegetables and corn bread. There's certainly nothing wrong with that. You know, a person can eat food that's too rich for him."

"Oh, come now, Mark. Surely you don't think an egg for breakfast now and then is too rich?"

"Gosh no. I love eggs. When I'm home my mama fixes me a couple every morning—if we have any in the icebox. But there's a verse that Reverend Ingram always quotes—he's the school president. He quotes it pretty often. It's about Daniel and his friends purposing in their hearts that they would not defile themselves by eating the rich food from the king's table. They challenged the king to give them water to drink and pulse to eat—"

74

"What to eat?"

"Pulse. I don't know exactly what it is, but Reverend Ingram says it's good plain food."

"Like biscuits and molasses?"

"That's right. Anyway, at the end of the test period Daniel and his friends were in good shape compared to the other young men who were eating meat and drinking wine at the king's table. Daniel's group had clearer eyes and firmer cheeks."

Clif reached over very suddenly and sort of gave my jaw a pinch. "Well, Mark, you've got some fine-looking cheeks yourself. I'll say that much for your plain diet."

"It really is a good diet. You know, sometimes a boy will get a package from home, all kinds of food—candy, sardines, stuff like that. Five or six of us get together and have what we call a feast. Gosh, we really eat. But the thing is that I always feel bad for two or three days after a feast. Sometimes I think a person would be better off to never eat any of that sweet stuff at all."

He sort of giggled. "But the trouble is, Mark, that the world's so full of sweet goodies that a man can't resist them."

"I guess so."

"Tell me, is it true that the authorities put saltpeter in the food at Wesley?"

I laughed, but I was a little uneasy. I wouldn't have minded talking to Floyd about saltpeter, but for some reason I kind of resented Clif asking a question like that. I said, "I don't really know. I've heard some of the older boys talking about it."

"What are they supposed to put it in?"

"Desserts mostly, I guess. I don't know anything about it for a fact, but there's this boy J. D. Stuckey—who's always talking about girls and worrying about his sex life, you know. And J.D. swears that the blackberry cobbler is the only thing they put it in. The cobbler is always the noon dessert on Sunday. J.D. really believes it too, because when we sat by each other in the dining hall he gave me his cobbler four straight Sundays."

"This J.D. sounds like quite a character."

"He's really pretty vulgar." I had seen him sitting in his room once, right in front of the open window, dumping about a ton of talcum powder on his private parts. Then he sat and rolled them around in his hand like he was admiring the family jewels or something.

"Oh, you don't like J.D.—even after he gave you all that blackberry pie?"

"He's all right, I suppose. Sometimes I think maybe a person just can't help too much being what he is. But I was glad when we changed tables again. They change every month."

"You must have eaten a lot of saltpeter by now."

"I guess so."

"Do you think it's affected you?"

I didn't know why I should start turning red, but I could feel my face getting hot. I'm no lily flower and I've certainly heard plenty and said a few things myself at the dorm. Yet, even though Clif was a nice sparkly friendly type, I was embarrassed.

I laughed a little bit. "I really don't think it has much effect on me at all."

"How can you tell? Do you ever get any girls at Wesley?"

"Oh, no. They definitely watch us too close for anything like that."

"Then how do you know it hasn't affected you?"

"I just know—that's all."

"Heavens, I've offended you again!"

"No, not really."

He reached over and patted the thigh muscles of my left leg. "You look tired, Mark. Why don't you take a nap?"

"That wouldn't be very polite of me. I mean, you picked me up so I could be company and talk to you. It wouldn't be right of me to just sit here and fall asleep."

"My, you do have a rigid little code, don't you? Well, Mark, you don't worry about me a bit. Take a little nap. If I get sleepy I always take a nap."

He turned on the radio and finally got a band playing for lunch at the Peabody Hotel in Memphis. They played some good tunes like "Goody Goody," "Alone," and "Dancing Cheek

76

to Cheek." Carl and I had seen the movie *Top Hat* at Christmas in Memphis. It was a wonderful picture, and I've dreamed about Ginger Rogers a few times since then.

That reminded me of Clif's questions about the saltpeter. In my ninth grade schedule of classes I'd had an hour of study hall that I had to spend in the upstairs auditorium every afternoon from two to three. The girls sat on one side of the hall and the boys on the other. Of course, there was supposed to be absolutely no talking—unless you got permission from the study-hall keeper to work on a problem or something for a few minutes with someone else. Well, across the hall on the same row with me was this girl Virginia Mae Ross. She was in the tenth grade. All the boys called her V. Mae. She was really a well-built girl. Many a time I'd be bent over a history book or working math, but over at the end of the row V. Mae would be showing lots of knee. I couldn't get my mind on what I was studying. Well, I guess I had my mind on what I was studying all right, but what I was studying wasn't in any of those books I was bent over. Sometimes V. Mae would look at me—when she knew Miss Hunter was reading or dozing off—and sort of try to stare me down. Then she would shift her legs around, I swear, like she didn't care how much of her she showed me. Just a few weeks ago she had even started getting permission from Miss Hunter to come over and study with me for ten minutes or so. Miss Hunter knew that V. Mae was in a higher grade, but I did have a reputation for intelligence. And, frankly, a person wouldn't have to be very smart to know more about algebra than V. Mae did.

When she sat seat to seat with me I would keep smelling her honey-skinned body. She didn't wear perfume or foo-foo water or anything like that, but she smelled clean and fresh and it did something to me. I suppose she washed her hair almost every day, because it was always bright and fresh-smelling. Naturally, on the occasions when we sat like that, Miss Hunter, after giving permission, would come alert like a bulldog sniffing for a cat. She'd be very sure to walk up and down that aisle a couple of times keeping an eye on us. But Miss Hunter must have known I wouldn't get fresh with V. Mae. She was at least three years older than me, and she dated several of the older boys. I mean *dated* in the Wesley sense, sitting together for a couple of hours on Saturday night and talking. I certainly knew I didn't have a chance with V. Mae, but it was still fun now and then to let my hand press alongside hers while we were looking at some problem in the algebra book. Sometimes, too, our heads would have to get pretty close together looking at a problem, and it was like we were breathing each other's air. That was wonderful, too. Now that the school year was over, I sure was going to miss looking down the row at those honey-pink knees.

I must have dozed off thinking about V. Mae. When I started waking up I became aware gradually that I was sitting way over at my side of the front seat, my head against the back of the green-plaid seat and the side of the car. The car was stopped. At first I thought we were at a filling station and that Clif was out of the car. But then I realized we were still in the country. Everything was very quiet. Clif was sleeping. He had stretched himself out a ways in the seat and was using my left leg for a pillow. He must have been as drowsy as I was, because he was sleeping very soundly.

I just had to move. I hated to bother Clif, but I got nervous knowing I couldn't even move without disturbing him—if you know what I mean. It was like somebody had locked me in a very small closet. I thought that if I couldn't move my legs right away then I'd just have to butt my head against that car door. So first I opened the door on my side very softly. Then I put my hands down very carefully around Clif's head and held it up while I eased my leg out from under. Then I let his head down to the seat and I got out of the car. I didn't slam the door—just closed it gently so that there was hardly any sound at all.

We were parked along a wide gravel shoulder away from the road itself. It looked as though some gravel trucks had been digging and hauling in that section. I did a few knee bends and bounced around a little to get my circulation going again. As long as there wasn't any dust being stirred up by passing cars, I also did some deep breathing. But my system was still sort of sluggish from the nap, so I started shadow-boxing. My daddy bought boxing gloves for Carl and me on my eighth birthday, and he taught us a lot. We even boxed exhibitions about once a year down at the wrestling matches in Jackson. There's no better all-round exercise than shadow-boxing. A person can get his energy circulating without feeling too bored in the process. With real imagination you can have a first-class boxing match all by yourself, and if you're feeling bad toward somebody you can imagine that's the opponent and really wham it to him. That's not really a good Christian attitude though.

Suddenly Clif raised his head and looked over the window. "What on earth are you doing?"

"Just shadow-boxing. I finished my nap and I was feeling cramped in the car."

"Goodness, I thought you had lost your mind!"

He sat up and rubbed his eyes.

I said, "Did you have a good nap?"

"Heavens, I don't know. Why, it's one-thirty! I must have slept for half an hour. And you didn't do too badly yourself, young man."

"I always get drowsy for a while in the afternoon."

"Well, I very seldom do. I hope I didn't bother you by using your leg for a pillow."

"Not at all. I hated to bother you by moving. But I just had to."

I got in the car. Clif pulled back onto the road and we headed on into Durant. Clif seemed very deep in thought. I glanced his way now and then. He was gripping the steering wheel very tight. I've never done much driving—in fact, none by myself—but there's no need to grip the wheel that tight. His brow was all wrinkled up too—making him look about forty years old instead of thirty.

He finally just started talking as though we'd had a conversation going all the time. "After I take care of my business in

Jackson, there's a young lady I have to see there. I hate to tell you this—a young fellow like yourself. The truth is that I'm married and have two fine children. We live up in Columbus. But there's this girl down in Jackson. I simply can't leave her alone."

I didn't know what to say.

He shook his head, as though the sorrow was just too much to bear, the shame of what he was doing. He said, "When you get my age, you'll understand how these things happen to a man."

It all seems pretty desperate. Here was this fine man with a young girl messing up his life, and there was Floyd back there with an old woman he couldn't leave alone. And in my mind V. Mae's legs and Geraldine's dark hair and that soft, moist patch seemed to be all mixed together. I guess all a man's life he just has to fight the women—about like Jacob wrestling that angel.

We caught one stop light in Durant, made our turn out to U.S. 51, and the white ribbon of concrete stretched out before us. At the city limits standing by a highway sign were two young men, one pretty short and the other very tall. Two suitcases stood in front of them, one with a bright red "M" hitting us in the face.

"Well, well, well," Clif said. "What have we here?"

FIVE

"The name is Belker—Dudley Belker," the short, slick-haired one said.

"Call him Dud, 'cause that's what he is, sure as hell," said the tall mole-chinned one. "I'm Tarzun—Will Tarzun."

"Will Tarzun," said Dudley Belker. "Hell, if Tarzun won't, who will?"

Clif sort of giggled. "Oh, him Tarzan, me Jane."

"No," the tall one said. "I'm Tarzun. You know—*zoon*, Tar*zoon* not Tar*zaan*."

Clif said, "Good! Wonderful! You Tarzoon, me June!"

Then they all laughed again. Ever since Clif stopped for them they had all been chattering like a bunch of blackbirds sitting in a cornfield. The short one, Dudley, was sitting with Clif in the front seat, and I was with Tarzun in the back. We had put their two suitcases in the trunk, but that still made it crowded for two grown people in the back—what with my grip and Clif's briefcases back there. But since I didn't really need too much leg room, it worked out fine with me sitting in the back.

Clif said, "I want you fellows to meet my young friend Mark Torrance."

"We didn't know his name," Dudley said. "But we've already seen each other back along the road."

"I'll bet the kid told him that," Tarzun said. "I'll bet he told

Clif to stop and pick up his old road buddies."

I said, "No, I didn't tell him anything of the kind. I figured Mr. Sharm could make up his own mind who he picks up."

Tarzun slapped his hand against the back of the seat. "You hear that, Dud? I told you the kid had the balls of a politician. Why, he could run for office and knock old Bilbo right out of the Senate!"

They had another good laugh at that. Clif sort of glanced back for a second and smiled. "Oh, I think Mark is just frank, that's all—just terribly frank. But tell me, where are you fellows heading?"

Dudley wasn't a bad-looking guy with his black slick hair. He said, "Well, Clif, put it this way. We've finished laboring in the fields of knowledge for a while and we got all summer to rest. No money to spend and all summer to spend it. Say, could I bum a cigarette, Clif?"

Clif passed his pack of Luckies to them, and when he got the pack again he took a cigarette himself. When Tarzun got the pack he held it in front of me for a second or two, and then he shook his head. "That's right, baby, you don't smoke. You're the boy from the Institute."

Dudley started laughing again. "He don't smoke and he don't chew, and he don't go with the gals that screw."

While they puffed away, I sat quietly dodging the ashes that came flying back when they would stick the cigarettes out the window for a second or two. Then they were all jabbering, each one trying to talk first. It seemed that the two of them were going over to Vicksburg to see their folks for a few days. Then they planned to bum over to Dallas and try to get jobs at the big Centennial. If that didn't work they were going on to California and look for summer work. I had heard a lot about California and the high wages paid out there. Last summer, in fact, Roscoe Swor, a guy about eighteen from Jackson, had hitchhiked out there. He sent one of his friends a card showing the Rose Bowl at Pasadena. Roscoe said on the card that he had taken a few laps around the football field the day before and that he was going to start work the next day at Paramount studios as an electrician's helper. We sure envied him, especially when we thought of all the fine movie stars he'd get to know. It made life in Mississippi seem pretty dull.

Suddenly at the end of a joke Clif really just sort of screeched and howled. The others laughed too, but all at once I noticed Will Tarzun winking at me. He had moved his head over to the side of the car so Clif couldn't see him through the rear mirror. Tarzun, with his hand on his knee, pointed toward Clif and rolled his eyes at me. I didn't get it. So in a few seconds Tarzun reached over and took the map out of my hand. He pulled out a pencil and wrote something on it, then handed the map back.

The note was on a clear spot in the gulf. It said, "Play it easy, kid. We got ourselves a live one."

He winked at me and I nodded my head. It certainly was about as fine a ride as we could have gotten. I was getting all the way home myself, and they'd have only forty miles to go when we got to Jackson.

With all that talk going on, a lot of it kind of dirty, I felt sort of left out. That was all right with me, because I could daydream or even doze and they didn't pay any attention to me. I'll say another thing too. Since I didn't have to keep up a conversation anymore, the time went pretty fast. From Durant to Pickens was thirty-eight miles or so, and even when we got stopped for five minutes in some kind of new bridge project south of Pickens we still seemed to make good time.

I kept my mind off all those dirty stories, but finally my thoughts were caught off guard. I mean, I couldn't blot out what was being said because I wasn't thinking strong enough about the particular subject in my mind at the time. And Clif was telling the story and his voice was getting so gaspy and screechy I couldn't help but notice. He said, ". . . and the girl says, 'I'm not going to eat that horrible-looking thing. Wait a minute.' She opens the refrigerator and takes out some chocolate syrup, which she pours on it. Then she drops a spoon of whipped cream and a sprinkle of pecans and finally she tops it with a nice red cherry. Then she says, 'Oh, that's much better. Now I can eat it.' And the boy says, 'The hell you will! Get one of your own. That's mine!' "

The way they all howled, it must really have been a good joke. We were getting close to Canton, which left only twenty miles to Jackson. I tried to think about home and how I was going to surprise Mama and Daddy. I wasn't going to call them to come get me in Jackson, no matter where Clif left me off. I would just get to the house the best way I could and walk in very casually. I have always liked to pull surprises like that.

Clif said, "There's a marvelous place about a mile on down. I stop there quite often. The beer's very cold and usually there are some pleasant people sitting around. Shall we have a cool one?"

Dudley said, "A cool one on a hot day! Man, you can't beat that. What say, Tarzoon?"

Tarzun said, "Tarzun like beer, June like beer." He leaned over and poked me with his finger. "Cheetah like beer?"

I smiled while they howled their heads off, but I didn't think it was especially funny. Clif turned the car into a gravel parking lot. The beer joint, which didn't look any different than a hundred others you could see along the highway, was plastered with tin beer signs such as "Schlitz," "Jax," and "Falstaff." Above the door in red neon was a little sign: BIG RED's PLACE. There was also another entrance marked LADIES, but I never figured this out, since it led right to the same place we ended up in.

Coming in from the bright sunlight, I couldn't seem to make out anything for a minute or two. But after I blinked my eyes a while I could see that there were some lights in the place. A dim fluorescent light hung over the bar, but there didn't seem to be much else except the glow from the different colored lights on the nickelodeon. But a person could see all right, especially after you'd been in there five or ten minutes.

A little section in front of the nickelodeon seemed to be cleared off for dancers, and in the long dark room were five or six booths and maybe ten tables. There was some kind of slot machine over at one wall, lit only by whatever lights it had. There had been four cars parked outside, and now I saw that two of the booths had customers, two ladies in one by themselves and an older-looking couple in the other one. A big red-headed man in a sport shirt stood behind the bar. When we finally settled down at a table, he stuck his head through a little opening in the wall behind him. "Hey, Yvette, you got business!" Then he smiled and nodded at us. "She'll be right with you, gentlemen."

The door from the kitchen opened and this girl walked over in a very hippy fashion. I suppose she wasn't bad-looking, but I didn't like her too much. She had a kind of painted look, if you know what I mean. That cotton dress of hers was sure skimpy thin, and you could see the outline of her bloomers whenever she leaned over. She wasn't really old or bad-looking, but she just had a look. If I messed with a woman like that, then I would *know* I was standing in the way of sinners.

She said, "What'll it be, boys?"

Dudley said, "Griesedieck. Would you like a Griesedieck, Clif?"

"Heavens, I'd love one!"

They started laughing, and Tarzun pounded the table like he was going to have a coughing fit.

Yvette looked pretty sour. "That ain't the way you say it. It's greasy *dike*, not—not that other."

"Dike, dick," said Dudley. "What's the difference?"

Clif said, "Now that's an utterly ridiculous comment." Then the three of them hooted again. I looked around to see if the people in the booths were upset by all the noise, but they didn't seem to be paying much attention.

Yvette said, "Well, we don't have no greasy dike anyway."

Tarzun said, "Oh, hell, honey, forget it. You wouldn't know if you had one right in your hand."

Yvette said, "Look, buddy, do you want Big Red to throw your ass out of here?"

It was sure embarrassing to hear a lady talk like that. I guess that was Big Red behind the bar. He stood like a bear, smiling at us, with his big hairy arms folded in front of him.

Clif smiled and patted Yvette's hand. "Oh, come now, Yvette. My friends were simply making a little joke. My, you've certainly got your dander up today."

Tarzun said, "Hell, my old dander gets up every morning."

They all started laughing again. I was afraid Big Red was going to come over, but then I saw his wide face showing teeth in a smile. Even Yvette laughed a little.

Yvette said, "That's pretty cute. The other was vulgar."

Dudley had been looking like he couldn't sit still, just dying to throw in a joke of his own. He said, "I like it when you smile, Yvette. Anything I hate to see is a good-looking girl with a sour puss."

Yvette gave Dudley a wink. "Sweet or sour—you'll never know about this one, sweetheart."

Clif said, "All this talk has made me terribly thirsty. Could I please have a beer, Yvette? Make it Schlitz."

Tarzun and Dudley ordered two Budweisers. Then Yvette looked at me. "I can't bring this one no beer. He's too young."

"Well, I don't drink beer anyway. I'd like an Orange Crush."

"Coke is what I got. You can have a Coke."

After she walked away, I took the nickel out of my pocket and put it on the table. "I can pay for my own, but I don't have any more money. I'm sorry."

Clif pushed the nickel back toward me. "Don't be absurd, Mark. You're my guest."

Dudley said, "I got another story, Clif. There's this man and his wife, see. He has this problem—weak kidneys, especially if he's been drinking late at night. So one Saturday night after this long party they fall into bed and the guy passes out. But the wife starts thinking maybe he will have trouble and wet the bed, so she decides to take a little action. She grabs a blue ribbon off the dresser and ties it round the end. Okay, the guy wakes up first thing in the morning and looks down there. Right away he starts shaking his wife and says, 'My God, honey, what a night! I don't even remember what happened, and look, I won first prize!' "

I excused myself and picked up my Coke from Yvette over by the bar. That filthy conversation was just too much. I don't believe even J. D. Stuckey ever stayed on one topic that long.

I walked over to this slot machine that I had noticed earlier. It was a game called Play Ball, one that I had played down in a Jackson drugstore once last summer. What made it such an interesting slot machine was that you didn't do the usual deal of shooting steel balls with a plunger and spring. The game was rigged just like a baseball field with players standing and holding their gloves to catch the ball if it rolled to them, dropping the ball into a hole for an out. Behind the players were slots at the back of the playing field, and you could do everything from hit a single to a home run, as well as fly out. The pitcher was like a little toy dressed like a ball player. He would lean back, the ball would pop up into his hand, and then in a second or two he would rock back and roll that ball towards the plate. Instead of a player standing there, a long stainless steel paddle, supposed to be the bat, covered the plate and when you pressed the button the paddle swung at the ball. It was real fun. I mean, there was some kind of skill involved since you had to time the ball just right in order to get a good hit. You could practice and pick out spots between the fielders and drive the ball right through. Of course, a lot of it was luck too. Anyway, you had to score ten runs before you started getting free games—one extra for each two runs from ten on.

It was sure a fine game, and it reminded me of the big board the *Clarion-Ledger* put on the outside of their building down in Jackson during the World Series every year. A big magnet was behind the board, and the operator would get the play from the wire service and move the magnet so that the ball on the field did exactly what the real play had been. A person in the street could use his imagination so that it was almost like being at the game. It was even better in some ways. I could remember some exciting games—like in 1932 when the Yankees really mopped up the Cubs in four straight. Almost every time you looked up, the bell on the scoreboard was buzzing—meaning a home run—and Babe Ruth and Lou Gehrig were trotting round the bases. I guess that one in 1934 was the one I won't forget. Old Dizzy Dean and his brother Paul had a tough fight against the Detroit Tigers of Mickey Cochrane, right until the very last game. Then the bottom seemed to fall out. The Cardinals had a big inning (even old Diz got two hits in that one inning) and it was all over. The crowd in the street in Jackson really got a kick out of that. Everybody liked Diz and, besides, St. Louis was much closer South than Detroit. I knew that Detroit had come back last fall and beaten the Cubs, but that was during my third week at Wesley. I was so homesick still that I didn't think I was going to live, much less worry about any ball game. Listening to the radio then would have made it worse. It would have reminded me of Daddy standing in that street in front of the big board, smoking his cigar and having a beer or a Coke, making little nickel and dime bets with the men around him on whether the next batter would get on base or not.

I did some skillful playing on this slot machine. The first time I scored sixteen runs and won four free games. Then I had a bad game, only scoring three runs, but I came back again in the next game and thought I never would stop scoring. It was like old Dizzy Dean and the Gashouse Gang against the Tigers.

Funny, after I won so much, I sort of lost interest. I went ahead and played my games out in a hurry. I picked up my empty Coke bottle and went back to the table.

Will Tarzun must have been roaming the jungle while I was gone, because he had found himself a perch over at the booth with the two women. They were drinking beer together, and Tarzun had them both laughing. I could just imagine the kind of joke.

When I sat down, Clif looked at me. "You must have done very well with your nickel, Mark. You played for thirty minutes."

I said, "I won a lot of free games. It's a baseball thing. I know a lot about baseball."

Dudley said, "Good. Tell us something, baby. We're sitting here dying to hear something about baseball."

Clif said, "Don't be rude, Dud. Just because Will's being ugly is no reason for you to be sarcastic with Mark."

I said, "Are you about ready to go on to Jackson, Clif?"

Dudley said, "Absolutely. He was just sitting here waiting for you to finish shooting marbles over there."

Clif said, "We'll leave very soon, Mark. I think, Dud, that you might just go over and tell Will that."

But Dudley had signaled Yvette for more beer. He stood up and put his hand on Clif's shoulder. "Take it easy. Simmer down, Clif."

Clif said. "Look over there at him. Just look! It's disgusting!"

I looked. Will Tarzun had his arm over the shoulder of one of the women, a kind of stringy-haired redhead.

Dudley said, "Now don't get excited. I'll go over and straighten him out."

When Yvette brought the three beers, Dudley picked up one of them and stood looking at the other two.

Clif said, "Just leave his here. I won't buy him beer if he's going to keep sitting over there."

Dudley said, "Come on, Clif, don't be small about this thing. I'll take Will's beer over. It'll make him ashamed of the way he's doing."

Picking up the other bottle, he turned and walked to the booth. For a minute he stood, talking to them. Then the other woman slid over in the booth and Dudley sat beside her.

Yvette stood at our table, looking at me. "How about it, buster? Do you want another Coke?"

"No" I said. "Do you have a Popsicle?"

"Jesus, honey."

"I don't really want anything."

She walked back to the bar, put her tray down, and started talking to Big Red. He leaned over to her, nodding his head. Now and then both of them would look in the direction of the booth where Dudley Belker seemed to be doing all the talking now. He didn't seem to be scolding Tarzun either, because the four of them were laughing. I figured Dudley was getting off another one of his refined-type stories.

Clif lit a cigarette from the short snipe that he had in his mouth, and then he smashed the butt down in the ashtray. I could smell all those dead butts—about the foulest smell there is. I wanted to take the ashtray over and dump it myself, since it looked like Yvette didn't consider that part of her duty.

Clif said, "I think it's scandalous that we brought you into this place, Mark. I don't know what I was thinking of. I'll bet you never saw such a degenerate place in your life."

Well, I had been in a couple of poolrooms in Jackson that I wouldn't exactly call the finest, most uplifting places in the world. Also, one Saturday night Mama had driven Carl and me across Pearl River into Rankin County, where there were a lot of bootleg places, and before we finally found Daddy I had seen the inside of two that looked like joints in that picture *Scarface*. People sat around drinking illegal whiskey, and there was a dice table with green felt and a guy with a stick shoving the dice around. That *Scarface* was sure a strong picture. All the kids in our neighborhood in Jackson had gone around for a long time calling themselves Camonte, which was the name of the character Paul Muni played. But I liked his buddy George Raft best, the way he was always flipping that half-dollar and sizing things up. I sure hated it at the last when Paul shot George—although you couldn't really blame him since, after all, George had been leading Paul's kid sister into sin. It seemed a terrible thing, though, that two such fine friends as Paul and George had to get busted up just over this little goofy-looking girl. She really wasn't good-looking at all.

Clif said, "I just hope, Mark, that you'll take a lesson here. See what bad qualities women like that can bring out in a man."

I nodded my head. It was too bad, but I think Clif was just jealous. If there had been three girls, he'd probably have been right over there himself. I didn't really see that he should blame Dudley and Tarzun, although those two are certainly not my favorite people.

I went through the door marked BULLS to use the toilet. When I was washing my hands, trying to breathe as little as possible in that place, I noticed a sign above the washbasin. It said, "Do you have a problem when things are looking up? See BIG RED for protection when in doubt. Prince's Turbans. Three for a quarter. The best for less." Underneath the sign was a smaller line, "Sold for the prevention of disease." Somebody had scratched *disease* out and had written in *pregnant women*.

When I walked out of the BULL room I saw right away that Clif was pretty mad. He was smoking his cigarette very rapidly, barely touching his lips with it and then puffing very quickly like a steam engine snorting real hard and short. A loud country music tune was blaring on the nickelodeon. On the dance floor Tarzun and Dudley had the two women and they were swinging and shaking all over the place. Dudley suddenly pulled the redhaired one real close to him, and there in front of everybody he slipped his right hand all the way down her back. He grabbed her bottom like a cat digging into a tree trunk.

Clif said, "What a disgusting filthy sight!" When he saw I was standing there, he said, "Come on, Mark, we're leaving. I won't be a party to such a spectacle."

Dudley must have caught sight of Yvette coming over to tote up the bill. He took the redhead by the arm and came rushing up to us.

Clif said, "I'm leaving, Dudley. I have to go."

Dudley dropped the redhead's arm and put his hand on Clif's shoulder. "Wait a minute, Clif. You didn't even meet the ladies yet."

Clif reared his head back and kind of sniffed the air. "Indeed?"

Dudley said, "This is Molly Lou, Clif. Molly Lou, my good friend Clif."

Molly Lou nodded. "Pleased to make your acquaintance."

The music stopped and Tarzun came up with the blonde woman. She was almost as tall as Tarzun, but not very good looking. In fact, I didn't think either one of the girls would win any prizes. Naturally, after I looked at their faces, both heavy with rouge and lipstick, I looked at their chests. Molly Lou was so bulky up there as to be floppy, sort of reminding me of my washwoman Mattie. The blonde, whose name was Jeanette, didn't have much of a chest at all. I guess that the reason she looked so caved in was because so much had gone into making those long legs. They all smiled and laughed, telling Clif that it was too early to leave, that they all had plenty of time to get where they were going.

Clif said, "Maybe you gentlemen have forgotten this young man here who has to get home to his parents."

Till then the others had paid as much attention to me as they would some small bug that crawled out of the walls. But now Dudley slapped me on the back. "Hell," he said, "Mark won't mind staying a little longer. We'll send out to a Seale-Lily store and get him a chocolate cone."

Jeanette said, "Molly Lou, isn't Mark the cutest thing?"

Molly Lou said, "He's a regular little tallywhacker."

I figured she was a regular little something too, but I didn't say it. Clif stood there, undecided about what to do. Finally he said, "Well, you can order me one more beer. I'll be back in just a minute."

He walked over to the BULL room and went inside. Tarzun and Dudley pulled more chairs up to the table. When the four of them were settled down over their beer like hogs at a trough, Molly Lou wanted to know what difference it made whether or not Clif wanted to leave. She grabbed Dudley's arm. "Jeff, honey, we got a car and we can go lots of places together."

Dudley said, "Damn that Jeff stuff. You know my name."

Jeanette said, "Tarzun don't mind if I call him Mutt, so how come you get high-horsed when Molly Lou calls you Jeff?"

I started laughing.

Dudley said, "Go play the marble machine, Pee Wee."

I laughed some more. Dudley wasn't really much taller than I was. And I thought Mutt was a pretty good name for Tarzun too. Dudley looked at me for a minute, then he turned back to the others. I was sitting in a chair that wasn't even up to the table, so they all just ignored me.

Jeanette said, "This Clif seems high-horsed to me. We got a car. So what do we care if he leaves?"

Tarzun said, "Because you're drinking his beer, baby."

Molly Lou said, "Oh, you boys are busted, huh? I figured you was hitchhiking just because you're college boys. But you're busted too, huh?"

Dudley gave that slick smile that matched his greased-down hair. "Don't start crowding the exits, kiddo. We got money. But we damned sure ain't going to drop our buckets in the well as long as the river is running high."

Molly Lou said, "Clif's got the money. I think I'll have a dance with him."

Jeanette said, "You ought to. Maybe you can get a rise out of him."

Tarzun said, "Any rise you get from him will have to be propped up." They all laughed at that. Then Tarzun said, "Play him along. Just keep him drinking. We'll come out of this in good shape—all of us."

Dudley squeezed Molly Lou's arm. "Roll me over in the clover and do it one more time."

Molly Lou said, "You really gin me, Jeff Baby."

Dudley said, "Piss on that Jeff stuff, kid. I told you once."

I stood up.

Tarzun said, "Where the hell you going, Sweetpea?"

Jeanette said, "Sweetpea. That's pretty good, Mutt."

Tarzun said, "Don't be going into the john and telling Clif

what you heard. You dummy up, huh, pal?"

"What?"

"Keep your lip buttoned." He sounded like Edward G. Robinson in a gangster picture.

Dudley said, "Just don't say anything to Clif about what we said."

I said, "What do you think I am? I don't go around tattling."

Dudley said, "That's fine. You're a good kid. You've got character."

Tarzun said, "Besides that—if you tell Clif, I'll bust your ass."

I walked over to the bar, leaving them laughing behind me. The Jax Beer clock behind the bar said two o'clock, but that was obviously wrong. Big Red said it was almost five o'clock. I thanked him and walked outside.

The sun was getting low in the west, but I blinked my eyes when I walked out of that dark hole. I went to the car and checked to see if my grip was still there. Clif had been so excited about getting that beer that he hadn't even locked up the car, but I guess that hadn't worried Tarzun and Dudley because their stuff was back in the trunk.

I reached inside and saw that Daddy's grip was still there. Then I stood facing that warm sun, feeling it soak into my skin through my clothes. I could smell the stale beer odor when the breeze blew from behind Big Red's. After a minute I started to practice my declamation, but I couldn't seem to get my mind on it right away. A lot had happened that day, and I was feeling a little bit lost, about half sick to the stomach. Yet I was only twenty miles from home. I could walk that if I had to. The thing was that I thought about Floyd and Geraldine, and then I found myself remembering that little wheezing Godbold baby. It seemed a dirty shame that a little infant like that should be fighting to get its breath while people sat around places like Big Red's and lapped beer like thirsty hound dogs.

I started on my declamation, but I had to stop in a minute because that older-looking couple that had been sitting inside in that far booth came out to their car and drove away.

I started again, and this time I went through the speech all the way. Then I practiced some of the real dramatic parts a few times. There was one line I really wanted to hit the audience with. I poured it on in the practice. "Ropes! Quivering, trembling bodies—dangling from the end of ropes!"

When I finished I thought I might have one more Coke, since I was thirsty from talking so strong. I walked back in, waiting by the door for a few seconds after I got back in. I didn't want to walk over a table in the dark.

Big Red and Yvette were standing by the bar, laughing and clapping their hands. Out in the middle of the dance floor Clif was standing, holding onto a bottle of beer and looking at the table where Dudley, Tarzun, and the girls were sitting. Clif was pretty drunk.

Dudley said, "Give us another one, Clif. Sing one more."

The others laughed and applauded.

Clif bowed his head, then straightened up. He started singing to the tune of "Strawberry Roan," but he had sure changed the words.

I was hanging round town a-spending my time,
Not making no money, not even a dime,
When a gal she walks up and she says I suppose
You're a heavy-hung stud from that bulge in your clothes.
Yessum, I says, I got a big one they claim,
And the whore never lived that I couldn't tame.

I turned and slipped back out the door. I wouldn't have thought Clif would make a fool of himself just to get one of those old trampy girls. I should have gone in there and told him they were just playing him for his money. But even if I told him, he probably wouldn't believe me. And I was afraid that Tarzun really might beat me up. Still, I should have told Clif. He had been very nice to me.

But I didn't. I got my bag out of the car and walked on into

Canton, then over to the south side of the town to catch a new ride. I just left Clif there, like a chunk of bacon dangling on a line with a bunch of red-clawed crawfish snapping at him.

While I walked, I kept wishing I was older and bigger. But most of all I kept wishing I had more guts.

SIX

JUST LIKE I figured he might be, there was Daddy standing at the beer bar in Edwards' Pool Hall. He was wearing his hard-rimmed straw hat with a pair of blue pants and a white long-sleeved shirt with the cuffs turned twice on each sleeve. His face and neck stood out brown and thick-muscled against the white shirt. The open collar made him look even bigger through the chest. Daddy's only about five-eight, but he has this tremendous chest and strong smooth-muscled arms.

Right now he was drinking Falstaff beer. I recognized a couple of the bricklayers he was talking to, but I guess they didn't notice me because I just walked right up and stood behind them for a couple of minutes. I could tell that Daddy had been having several beers. A lock of his dark hair was hanging down almost over one eye. Whenever he drinks a lot, he always seems to lose track of that sprig of hair, and bingo, it falls right out from under his straw hat.

Daddy said, "Well, by God, there's got to be something done—one way or the other."

Corley Webb said, "We got to stand together, Carl. We don't have a chance unless everybody holds what he's got."

Daddy said, "My trouble is I don't have a damned thing to hold. Union or not, I've got to start working damned soon."

Bud Stout said, "We know, Carl. Everybody's feeling the pinch."

A dark, very husky man with a gap between his front teeth said, "The leadership here is lousy. These officers wouldn't make a pimple on a good leader's ass. Hell, they run bums like Lib McGraw out of Birmingham."

Daddy said, "Lib's all right, but I'm tired of the talk. We make a lot of talk about the union, and the others go out and take what jobs there are."

The big man said, "We ought to whip the goddam scabs till they can't walk. Make them think twice before they scab on honest union men."

Daddy said, "Keep your goddam shirt on, Shaw. There's no reason to blame a man when he takes work so his family won't go hungry."

Shaw said, "Hell, you people down here take it too easy."

Daddy still hadn't turned my way. I caught his sleeve, and when he saw me standing there, he was so surprised he didn't know what to say, just stood there with a big grin on his face. Then he leaned over, sort of hugging me to him, and then—as if he remembered we weren't at home but in that public pool hall—he caught hold of my right hand, like we were shaking, and just kept squeezing it. I could smell the beer on him, but there was also his personal smell, a kind of manly smell that was different from my own but which I always liked.

He said, "What are you doing home?"

I told him I was exempt and that Reverend Ingram had said it would be all right for me to come home for the week. I didn't mention the money we owed the school. And I didn't tell him I had hitchhiked. I was saving that for a surprise when I had him and Mama together.

He said, "You mean you've already been up to the house?"

"Oh, sure. I found it all right. The downstairs door was open so I went on up. I even took a bath."

"Your mama still hadn't come home when you left?"

"I didn't stay at the house over fifteen minutes. I thought you might be down here."

Daddy patted me on the back and introduced me to the men I didn't know—including the big one, Shaw—while I was nodding and shaking hands with those I did know such as Corley Webb and Bud Stout.

Bud Stout said, "You want a beer, Mark?"

Daddy laughed. "Thank God this one don't have a taste for the damned stuff. But you ought to see his brother. Carl's not quite fifteen and he started on home brew when he was ten years old."

Bud slapped Daddy on the back. "Carl got more than just his name from you, didn't he?"

The others laughed. Mr. Edwards, who was working the bar, came up and asked if I wanted a Dr. Pepper. I said I'd rather have an Orange Crush. I was mighty happy to see that he had one—a nice cold one too. I had been thirsty for a cold Orange Crush ever since Big Red's Place.

Daddy said, "This boy is the smart one. You hear what he said? He won't have to take examinations. Already passed the damned course. Thirteen years old and done passed the ninth grade."

Bud Stout said, "That's a boy with brains all right."

Corley Webb said, "When you going to start making a bricklayer out of him, Carl?"

Daddy said, "I'll knock him in the head if he ever thinks about laying brick. This boy is going to wear a shirt and tie and watch the poor bastards work in the sun."

In a few minutes we left the pool hall and started walking up Capitol Street. We had a pull uphill about eight blocks, but it was good to walk with Daddy like that. Lights in all the stores were blazing, and there was a floodlight on the Old Capitol building up at the head of the street. I told Daddy that I sure liked the location of the apartment. We were at the top of the ridge, a couple of blocks north of the Old Capitol. Behind those two blocks the land dropped off sharply to the east, where beyond the fairgrounds and the thick growth of greenery was the

Pearl River. The G.M. and N. station, the Old Capitol, and the ball park in the fairgrounds were jammed right together. Many a home run ball over the right field fence had ended up by a Civil War cannon or bouncing along the railroad tracks.

I remembered one spring when the Pearl River went out of its banks and backed up all the way to the ridge, completely covering the fairgrounds and the ball park. It seemed strange to look at all that muddy water covering a place that connected in your mind with ball games, merry-go-rounds, auto races, and big clusters of fair-going people.

When we got to the big yellow two-storied house I could see the '32 black Plymouth sitting at the side entrance, which went upstairs.

I said, "Look. Mama's home."

Daddy said, "It's about time."

She came out from the kitchen as soon as she heard us on the stairs. I ran to her, throwing my arms around her waist. My mother is big, almost as tall as Daddy, and a heavy woman without being too fat. She takes real good care of her face, always putting cream on it at night. She has very smooth skin and green eyes. Although she's twenty years younger than Daddy, I have never thought of there being much difference in their ages. In fact, if Mama hadn't mentioned it to Daddy once when they were having a little argument, I never would have thought about it. For a man fifty-eight years old Daddy is in darned good shape. He still has jet-black hair with just a trace of gray at the temples. Even though his stomach sometimes hangs over his belt, especially if he's too relaxed from drinking, he still looks like a strong physical specimen.

I could hardly get enough of hugging Mama. She sort of reminded me of sweet flowers, and the smell of her was the same way the house always started to smell, clean and sweet, after we'd been there for any length of time. The smell was soapy, not perfume. Mother seldom wore any perfume. She didn't need to.

We walked on back to the big room which had their bed in it

as well as the dining room table. A large second bedroom, for Carl and me, was up the hall past the bathroom.

Mama said, "Are you hungry, honey?"

I told her I thought I might eat a little something.

She said, "What time did the bus get in?"

"I didn't take the bus. I hitchhiked."

"Hitchhiked?"

Daddy was taking off his shirt, but he stopped midway. "What's wrong with you, Mark? You've got no business out on the road little as you are. It's a wonder somebody didn't knock you in the head."

"Why would they want to do that? I didn't have any money."

I told him I didn't have any trouble at all, but I didn't tell all the things that had happened. I mean, if I made it sound too strange they would never let me do it again.

Mama said, "I thought maybe you borrowed bus fare from the school, but now I see. Mr. Ingram told you to hitchhike."

"That's right. He knows I'm no baby. Anybody can read a map and find the way home."

Daddy said, "He told you to hitchhike? That sonofabitch must be crazy!"

Mama took the letter from the table and gave it to Daddy. He started looking for his glasses. He gets a fifty-dollar pension from the VA for bad eyes and high blood pressure. But he has to be careful. Once when we were riding downtown on the bus, Carl was sitting next to Daddy, and I was in the seat behind. Carl was reading a *Ring Magazine,* and all at once he stuck it in front of Daddy's face to show him how Nat Fleischer had ranked the top ten heavyweights. Daddy pushed the magazine away quick. He said, "Don't ever show me anything to read. You know I can't see." Then he looked around very carefully to see if anyone had seen Carl showing him the magazine.

I was going to read Mr. Ingram's letter for him, but Mama said to let him read it for himself. He finally did, and when he finished he took the glasses off and looked at Mama. He said, "That sonofabitch!"

I said, "That's twice you've said that about a man of God."

Daddy looked at Mama. "We'll talk about this later."

Mama said, "Well, it's no secret from Mark. Old Ingram told him why he was sending him home."

I said, "He sure did. Eighty-four dollars."

Mama said, "Did you tell your brother?"

I said, "No, ma'am. I didn't want to worry him when there was nothing he could do. I just told him I was going home because I was exempt."

Daddy went over to the table and pulled a chair around. He started staring out the window. Finally he looked around. "Fix Mark some eggs. He's hungry."

Mama moved into the kitchen. "Well, eggs is about all there is to fix."

Daddy half jumped out of the chair. "Goddamit, I know that!"

"I just thought I'd remind you."

"There's no use going to any trouble," I said. "I'm not really hungry."

Mama said, "Piddle! You know good and well you're hungry. Don't let your old bear of a daddy upset you."

Daddy said, "Just don't act like I don't know there's nothing to eat here!"

Mama said, "Maybe Mark don't want eggs. He could walk around to the Crystal and get three of those little hamburgers and a milk shake."

I said, "That sounds good."

Daddy said, "Have you got any money?"

"No, sir."

Mama said, "Give him a quarter, Carl."

Daddy reached into his pocket and fished around. Finally he slapped a dime on the table. "Clara, give him fifteen cents."

Mama looked at the dime as if she never saw one before. "My God, Carl, you mean to tell me that's all you have left from that two dollars you had this morning? Well, I'll bet *you're* not hungry. Your stomach is too loaded with beer."

Daddy's face turned red. He curled his lip, and I could see the teeth in the upper plate that he had bought a few years ago when he had that good Courthouse job. Daddy was very proud of his teeth. Mother told him one day that when he was dying the last thing he'd do would be check to be sure his teeth were in.

He said, "All right. I had a few beers. And I bought Bud Stout a couple."

Mama said, "You'd need to buy him a couple of cases to fill him up. Well, if you're going to buy beer for every bum of a bricklayer then your boy will have to do without hamburgers."

Daddy said, "You had a few dollars last week. Where's that gone?"

Mama said, "I had to fill the car with gas."

She walked into the kitchen and took the dark skillet from the oven.

Daddy said, "Gas? Gas? Gas to go where? You put enough gas in that car every week to go to California and back."

Mama just ignored Daddy. She put on a pot of coffee while she was making toast and scrambled eggs. Daddy just stared off out the window at that long stretch of fairgrounds parking space and the high trees toward the river. After a while he got up and pulled some rolls of blueprints from the chest of drawers. Then he sat down at the table with a pad and pencil in his hand. After a minute he jumped like somebody had stuck him with a pin. He ran to the window and pulled the shade down.

Mama said, "Do you think there's a VA man over in that tree?"

"If there is, then the bastard had a nice climb for nothing. One day I'm going to forget myself and that will be the end of that fifty dollars a month."

"That might be a blessing. Then at least you wouldn't have to be scared everytime you get a job."

"I'm not scared. I got to work. By God, a man don't have to

say he's totally blind to get a damned fifty dollars compensation. But if they get a chance to call me up again, they might try to cut my payment down."

Mama put the steaming eggs and toast and coffee on the table.

Daddy said, "Don't eat so fast, boy. You'll get indigestion."

Mama put a cup of black coffee in front of him. "I know this won't do you as good as Falstaff beer, but you might try it."

Daddy looked up from his numbers. I thought at first he was going to get mad again, but after a few seconds he smiled at her. "You know, Mark, your mama has learned a lot in the seventeen years since I took her out of that Delta cotton patch. The first time we took the ferry across the river at Baton Rouge she started waving and crying, 'Goodbye, goodbye, old United States.'"

Mama said, "Carl, I wish you'd stop telling that lie." But she smiled.

She walked around and stood at the end of the table where Daddy was working. After a minute or so, she said, "Why do you keep figuring? You've been through that thing ten times already."

He slapped the pencil down and got up from the table. He put his hand on one of our big electric fans that was sitting on top of the chest of drawers. He switched the fan on and off a couple of times, and then left it off. We had two of those big fans. In the summer I would reach the point where I could hardly go to sleep without one of those fans blowing on me. It wasn't always that I liked the coolness so much, because late at night—even in the summer—the air became fairly cool and moist, sometimes even chilly. But I just got used to that hum. If Mama or Daddy came in to turn the fan off Carl and me, I would always wake up right away, even if they made no noise at all. I always missed that hum as soon as it stopped.

Daddy finally said, "How much did Hunt and Whitaker give us on these fans last time?"

Mama said, "Five dollars. Five dollars for both of them."

"That won't do us much good."

"It sure won't."

Daddy shook his head and walked over to the table. He picked up the cup of black coffee and took a long gulp of it. Then he sat down and grabbed the pencil again.

Mama said, "Carl, if you start that figuring again, I'm going to run stark raving mad out into the streets."

He said, "I have to keep figuring, trying to see what I can cut it to and still make it pay."

Mama said, "You're just trying to talk yourself into doing it."

"If I do I'm sure going to wish like hell I had that pistol out of the pawnshop."

"Poo! I didn't hear of them jumping on anybody yet."

"I can take care of myself. But I can't whip four or five at a time. I could use that pistol."

"You'll have the money to get it Saturday—if you work."

"I just hope it's not rusty from being in that hockshop three years."

"You've paid enough interest on that thing you could have bought one of Al Capone's machine guns."

"I never should have hocked it in the first place. For three years it's been like something was missing inside me. But I'll have it back on Saturday!"

Mama watched with bright quick eyes while he paced back and forth like one of those lions in the cage at Livingston Park Zoo. The more he walked, the more his chest puffed out. Pretty soon there wasn't a sign of stomach hanging over his belt. I guess if he'd had a long tail he'd have been lashing that back and forth too.

Suddenly he stopped pacing. He looked at Mama. "Are you telling me to do it?"

"I'm not telling you anything, Carl. I think you know what we have to do. God knows I'm tired of thinking we got to run to

Memphis or Baton Rouge every time you need a job."

"Old Corley said they'd probably put me up for vice-president of the union next month."

"Before you take that job find out how much salary they plan to give you. Then see if that will—"

"It wouldn't be much, you know that. But it's a kind of honor."

"Good. See if old brother Ingram up at Wesley will take that honor and put it on your boys' bill."

Daddy picked up the phone and told the operator some number. After a few seconds he said, "Hello, Mr. Maley, this is Carl Torrance. . . . Yes, I'm all right. Did you get anybody to run that brickwork for you yet?"

Mama said, "Pick up some dishes, Mark. Bring them in the kitchen."

She ran some hot water into the sink, then picked up a few other cups and glasses and slipped them into the suds. When I brought in the rest, she said, "Get a rag and dry for me."

I waited for each dish and glass to drain a little before I polished them with the rag.

Mama said, "I'll bet you've grown two inches since Christmas. Do your clothes still fit?"

"The things I got last summer are a little small, but Carl's been wearing them. What I really need is shoes."

"Shoes? Those shoes look all right."

"I took care of them. But now they're too small. They hurt my feet."

"They're size eight!"

"I know."

"My God, your daddy don't wear but a nine! You're the biggest-footed young boy I ever saw."

"Coach Williams said I was going to be a big man when I grew up. He said big hands and big feet were a sure sign."

"If your daddy gets that job, we'll buy you some clothes and shoes before you go back for the contest."

It would sure be nice to walk out on that stage with a brand new pair of shoes.

Mama said, "You and Carl Junior were anxious to get back to Wesley when you came to Memphis at Christmas. Don't you even miss your mama and daddy anymore?"

She sort of stopped her dishes and just looked at me. I put my right arm around her waist and hugged her. "Sure, we both miss you a lot. But it never has been as bad as that first month back in September. Honest, a couple of times I thought I was just going to have to run away from there—either run away or just lie down and die."

"But you never feel that way anymore?"

"Mama, the thing is that we miss you and Daddy all the time, but we have to learn to do without you. No, I don't mean—what I mean is that we know you can't be there, so we get used to it. Gosh, there are some really small kids down in the junior dorms. I mean, they're third and fourth graders. They even get used to being away from their folks."

"I know. Some of them are awful pitiful kids, I imagine. They come from broken homes."

"Broken?"

"Their parents have separated."

"I never had thought about that. It's pretty sad. But I guess it's true."

Mama finished wiping off the stove, and then she wrung out the cloth and hung it over the stove to dry. "I know the school has helped both of you. It's helped you grow up a lot faster. But there's something about that too. I hate to see y'all grow away too fast. You'll both be gone soon enough—in just a few years now."

Daddy came into the kitchen with the sheet of figures in his hand. "It's all settled. I'm going to do that job for old Maley."

"What can you make out of it?"

Daddy looked at the sheet. "Not much. Maley won't pay but three hundred, and he wants it done by the end of the week."

"For a man who had a hard time getting bricklayers he's in a big hurry all of a sudden."

"Well, he's got a few scabs nosing round for the job now. But most of them come from out of town. He's afraid they ain't good. But he was still about ready to give the job to somebody else. Let's see, check my figures. Fifty hours of work for three bricklayers at seventy-five cents an hour, that's $112.50. Two laborers is fifteen apiece for thirty dollars, one mortar man twenty dollars. That's $162.50 all told, leaving me with about a hundred-forty for my own work and the contracting—if I can get it finished by the end of the week."

"Yes, and if you can get any bricklayers to work for six bits an hour."

"That's all fixed too. I got three men all right. Nigger Ward and two others."

Mama put a little squirt of Jergen's Lotion in her palm and started rubbing her hands together. She looked at Daddy, a little frown cutting across her forehead. "I don't know about that, Carl. I just don't know."

Daddy said, "Clara, what you know or don't know won't make a damn now. I talked to Ward. They're coming to work."

"You're liable to have trouble enough like it is. They start calling you 'nigger lover' too it's going to be worse."

Daddy's face reddened. He threw his chest out again. "Damn the union, ain't that right! Didn't you just stand in there and say that the union wasn't putting any grub on my table? Didn't you?"

"That's right! Throw the whole thing up to me. Say I'm the one who's making you do it."

Daddy pranced around some more. "Nobody's making me do a damned thing! Ward and his men will work for six bits, and all the union people will want a dollar. The less I pay out, the more I have left. And, hell, we're going to owe old Ingram up there eighty-four dollars." Daddy reached over and felt my right arm up by the muscle. "You think you're strong enough to do a man's work, Mark?"

"You mean I can go out on the job and really work?"

"You always been too young before. But this is good a time as any to see what the work is like. You be a laborer and I'll pay you five dollars."

"Gosh, that would be fine! I can take off my shirt and get a good tan right there on the job. And I'll probably get pretty strong handling those bricks."

Daddy reached into the closet and brought out his tool box. He checked his trowels, the levels, a couple of brick hammers and chisels, and a ball of heavy white cord. He checked through the stuff for a couple of minutes. Then he got up and went in the other room.

I heard the fan cord being pulled from the plug. Then he came back and took the other cord loose from the fan beside their bed.

Mama said, "Do you have to do that?"

"You got five dollars without hocking them?"

"I guess not. On your way back stop and get some ham for your lunch. And a loaf of bread and some sausage. Maybe a few apples and oranges or bananas."

"Get bananas, Daddy." I loved banana sandwiches, made with mayonnaise and peanut butter.

Daddy said, "You want to go to the pawnshop with me, Mark? You can come in with me. You can take a look at the pistol when I check it to see if it's getting rusty."

Mama said, "He's not going anywhere except to bed. This boy's been on the go ever since daylight. And he's got to get up early in the morning if he goes to work with you."

Daddy nodded. "That's right, I forgot. Get your rest, boy. Tomorrow's work day."

"But I want to see the pistol."

"Don't worry. I'm going to get it out from the shop this weekend."

Mama said, "Well, you're not going to get those fans in to-night unless you hurry."

I helped him take the fans down to the car. With those big

bases they were hard to handle but not really heavy.

After he got in the car, Daddy squeezed my arm. "I'm proud you don't have to take those examinations, Mark. Keep studying hard like that. Go to college and be a lawyer. You won't have to work the way I do for a living."

I went upstairs and got ready for bed. It was good to be back with the folks again, good to smell those fresh sheets and lie there with my foot moving from one cool spot to another. After a few minutes Mama came in and kissed me.

"Good night, honey. You ought not have hitchhiked like that, but I'm glad you came home. Get a good sleep."

"Mama, is Daddy going to be a scab?"

"It don't make any difference what those men call him, Mark. He's doing what he thinks he has to do—for you and me and your brother."

"Oh, sure, I know that. But you don't think those other bricklayers will jump on him, do you?"

"Your daddy comes from a line of people that wouldn't think a thing in the world of fighting a bunch of tigers. Your daddy can take care of himself." She laughed softly. "If he gets that pistol out of hock Saturday, he'll scare half these bricklayers to death if the mangy devils jump on him. Don't you worry about that."

But I did keep worrying. I thought about Will Tarzun and what he'd said to me. I thought how I couldn't do anything about it. And now here was my daddy in trouble and there didn't seem to be much that I could do about that. I thought about that big guy Shaw down at the pool hall, the way his brown hands and fists had looked.

It had been the longest and yet the shortest day of my life. I started saying my prayers. First off, I thought of the Godbold baby and I prayed that his lungs would get stronger the more of that dusty air he breathed. I hated to think of that little baby dying. Then I thought about Floyd and Geraldine and her mama. I wasn't sure exactly what to pray there, but I asked God to take care of them. I said a word for Clif Sharm, and even though I wasn't too enthusiastic I also prayed that the Lord would convert Dudley and Tarzun, but I couldn't really see that people like them would add much to life in Heaven. I'd rather have some of those heathen Chinese and Africans than them. I asked blessings on Mama and Daddy and Carl. I was starting to miss Carl quite a bit. This was the first night I could remember in my life that Carl hadn't been sleeping in the same room with me. I didn't want to be silly or anything, a man who had hitchhiked a hundred miles that day, but I couldn't help missing him. Finally I said, the way Carl and I always did, "Good night to the world." I could just hear Carl saying it back to me up there at Wesley. And I could hear John Poole over in his corner bed, trying to sound tough, saying, "Good night to Mark and Carl. And screw the world." Just before I dropped off to sleep, although I tried to push it completely out of my mind, I remembered the way my fingers had felt in Geraldine's hair-patch.

SEVEN

I CAME awake in the early morning, not yet daylight, with Mama shaking my shoulder. It seemed to be the middle of the night, and I lay there, hating to move, like some kind of chicken egg that knew it was time but refused to hatch itself. Mama finally yelled to Daddy, who was shaving in the bathroom, "Make that boy stir around, Carl!" Then Daddy was leaning over me, the smell of shaving lather on his face, saying, "Up and at it, boy! Get up, get up, get on the rock, it's not daylight but it's six o'clock." He rustled me around, and the next thing I knew I was out of bed, the floor cold against my warm feet. While Daddy finished shaving in the bathroom washbasin, I leaned over the tub and splashed cold water over my face and neck and back. Daddy growled at me to keep the water off the floor.

In just a few minutes the eggs and sausage were steaming on the plates. Mama was already feeding lots of food—just like that payday Saturday was already in her pocketbook.

When Daddy finished his coffee, he glanced at the front page of the paper.

I said, "Daddy, do you want me to pull that shade down?"

Mama laughed. Daddy said, "Don't worry about it, Mark. I can see there ain't no VA man up there this morning." Then he looked at the paper. "It looks like this Landon is going to be it for the Republicans. Who the hell ever heard of the man?"

Mama said, "Look at Mark. He's as sleepy as he can be. I think he ought to go back to sleep. A thirteen-year-old boy has no business out on a brick job."

Daddy didn't even glance up from the paper. "It will do him good, make a man out of him."

Daddy kept calling out news from the paper, but Mama told him to hush because the Roaming Cowboys were coming on the radio.

Daddy said, "Cowboys, hell. A Mississippi cotton patch is about the most those old boys ever roamed in."

Mama said, "You just don't appreciate good fiddling, Carl."

When the cowboys started singing their song about "nowhere to go and nothing to do," Daddy snorted again. "One of these days they'll have somewhere to go. Uncle Sam will put a gun on their shoulder and send them to get Mussolini."

The job was out in the rich section of North Jackson on Council Circle. The drive out took ten minutes or so. I sat in the back seat, sniffing the air, watching the early morning haze gradually clear as the sun came up strong and hot. Mama dropped us off at the job a little before seven. I stretched myself, feeling a little lazy. I hated to think about working, but at the same time I knew I would feel good once I got started. Daddy had told me to take it pretty easy that first day.

While Daddy talked to Ward and the other two Negro brick-layers, the mortar man started sloshing the sand and cement and lime in the mixing trough. The two Negro laborers began piling stacks of brick in several different places. I felt a little strange when I first realized that Daddy and I were the only white people on that job. I remembered what Mama had said about people—those union people—might call him "nigger lover." But after I started working I forgot all about that. Later, I did notice that every time a car would slow down and the driver would take his time looking at the men or the job, Daddy would raise his head and peer out over his glasses. If he didn't know the man or if it just seemed to be some curious guy playing street superintendent, then Daddy would turn back to work as quick as he could.

Daddy could sure run a job so that everybody worked as fast as possible. I just didn't see any wasted motion at all. It took Daddy and Ward a little while to build up the corners of that brick veneer house, but once they got set you could see those brick really start to fly. There were two long stretches, about thirty feet each, broken by a chimney that Ward built practically by himself. When those corners were up, Daddy took over one stretch while Ward's two men, Roberts and Brewer, did the other. Darned if Daddy didn't just about beat them every time. Roberts and Brewer would make the sweat fly, but at the end of each row they would shake their heads and say they never saw a brick-laying man like Daddy. Old Ward, building up that chimney, would laugh and say that these young squirts just never worked with a real first-class bricklayer before.

But I really got a kick out of Roberts and Brewer. Roberts was heavyset, built very strong, with a flashing gold tooth in the middle of his mouth. He reminded me of a picture of Jack Johnson that I saw once in *Ring Magazine*. Brewer was a little leaner, but he was strong too. He had a funny way of moving his feet around while he laid brick, shuffling like a fighter in the corner before the bell rings. Sometimes the two of them would sing while they worked. I guess it wasn't what you could really call singing, but at least they'd start saying things in rhythm, especially when they were working that long stretch trying to keep up with Daddy. The trowels zipped the mortar and klonked the bricks, and they would sing:

> *Run those brick, slap 'em right down.*
> *Run those brick, gotta go to town,*
> *And see my honey in a nice silk gown.*

They would chant this over and over again, sometimes mixing in other words, but they kept it pretty clean. Once Roberts stopped and asked Daddy, "Mister Carl, you gonna make a bricklayer out of your boy?" Daddy said, as usual, that he'd knock me in the head if I ever looked like I wanted to lay brick. Roberts slapped his hands together. "Woo—eee! Your daddy telling you right, boy. Sure 'nuff telling you right!" Then he sang some more, with Brewer joining him after the first time through:

> *Say, Mister Carl, what you gonna do*
> *When your boy wants to lay hisself a brick or two?*
> *Knock him in the head, boys,*
> *Knock him in the head!*
> *Mister Carl raised his boy to have a feather bed.*

Daddy laughed then, the sweat running down his undershirt into the old khaki trousers he worked in. The part of his back and his arms not covered by the undershirt started to get a red-brown in the sun. I knew he felt tired, because his stomach was sagging over his belt. Now and then, at the end of one of those races with Roberts and Brewer, he would stop and breathe deep and shake his head for a few seconds. Then he'd start right back again. I thought about his eyes and his high blood pressure, and I wished that I was big enough and smart enough to take his place and let him just sit in the shade.

We all got to sit in the shade for thirty minutes at noon. Mama drove up with sandwiches and bananas and—best of all— big quart fruit jars filled with iced tea. It was the best food I ever tasted. Daddy sat there in the car and ate his lunch, but I took mine over and sat with the other workers. I told them that I was going to be in the declamation contest at Wesley the next Monday. They probably didn't want to hear the speech, but when they asked me I said it for them. When I finished stomping up and down, yelling about those quivering, trembling bodies dangling from the end of ropes, they all clapped their hands. Ward said, "Don't you see now what his daddy said, Roberts? This boy going to make a shyster lawyer."

I got pretty tired that first day, but I kept going. I liked the smell of the lumber shavings left by the carpenters, the feel of the fresh orange-brown dirt turned up along the foundations, and the sharp cleanness of the lime and mortar smell. And I could feel myself getting stronger with every brick I picked up. I read somewhere that Jimmy Foxx got his strong wrists milking cows as a boy, and I hoped that handling those brick would make me strong enough to someday be the leading home run hitter of the American League. My muscles ached, my fingers getting so sore that sometimes I felt that I just couldn't pick up another brick. But I made myself keep going. I didn't want Ward and them to think I was just a weak white kid.

Then, on Thursday afternoon, with everything going so fine, I stepped on a nail sticking up from a piece of lumber. I was half sick at the stomach when I raised my leg and that board followed like some kind of ski stuck to my foot. I held my breath and jerked the board as hard as I could. It came loose fast, but I still imagined I could feel the inside of my heel tearing as the nail came out.

It didn't hurt much, but Ward shook his head and rolled his eyes a little. He said, "You get hurt like that and don't bleed outside, that's a bad thing. That means inside bleeding—the ugly kind with the poison staying inside you."

Daddy ran water over the foot, but the nail hole still didn't bleed much. Then Daddy took a small stick for a paddle and spanked my heel some, but that didn't make it bleed either. Daddy looked at the nail and figured it must have gone into my heel almost an inch. He said I'd better go up and see the doctor. There was one about two blocks away on North State Street, a small office in a neighborhood cluster of stores. Daddy asked if I wanted Ward to drive me up there. I said there was no reason for anybody else to stop working. I knew Daddy had been pushing everybody as hard as he could to finish the job on time.

I kept my other tennis shoe on, and I walked on the ball of my foot and my tiptoes to the doctor's office. There wasn't much to the treatment. The doctor made me get down on my knees with my foot turned up behind me. Then he told me to grab the rung of the chair, and instead of hollering, to hold that rung as tight as I could so that any pain I felt would go out through my fingers and hands. He showed me a long hollow needle, like something used when a football is pumped up. He said he would stick that needle in my heel and pour some medicine down it. That way the infection would get covered by the medicine. He asked me if I had been shot for tetanus. I said I didn't know. He said that folks called it lockjaw. I said I still didn't know. I thought he was trying to sell me something extra, so I told him to just pour that medicine down that little pipe and everything would be fine. I grabbed the rung of that chair when he stuck that needle in my heel, twisting it as he did. The sweat popped out on my face, and I'll bet I left some permanent fingerprints on that chair rung.

He slapped a little gauze bandage on my heel and told me to stay off my foot for the rest of the day at least. The charge was two dollars. I told him my daddy would stop by and pay him on Saturday. He said not to worry about that, because if a two-dollar fee was all he ever lost he'd be richer than old man Rockefeller.

I walked on back to the job and told Daddy what the doctor said about me staying off my foot. Since it was only two-thirty and Mama wasn't supposed to come after us until five-thirty, Daddy gave me a nickel and I caught the bus back to the house. We lived only a block from the bus stop.

The car was there, but Mama might have been taking a nap, so I opened the screen door very quietly down at the bottom of the stairs. Then, from up in the hallway I heard her talking on the telephone. I decided to wait till she had finished; then I would jump up and surprise her. I have always liked to surprise people. That's one habit I'm sure going to try to break.

I sat on the bottom of the dark stairs waiting for her to finish talking. I took off my tennis shoe to see if the heel had ever done any bleeding, especially since the doctor had jammed that miserable needle up there. But the bandage was still white.

Upstairs I heard Mama laugh, soft and musical as the song of a bird. She said. "I know you're the craziest fool in this world." Then her laugh bubbled up a little more. I didn't know who she was talking to, but there were several of her friends that acted like the craziest women in the world.

Mama said, "All right, but I'm not sure. I don't know what time Carl will get through Saturday."

That's the truth, I thought. If everybody doesn't keep moving at top speed out there, he may not finish till Saturday night. And every extra hour after noon is going to cost him some of that profit he's figuring on.

Mama said, "All right. I can't get away later and you can't get away now. We'll just have to wait."

I wished she'd finish the conversation.

She said, "You talk like I don't want to see you. Don't be such a fool."

You get two women on the phone, my daddy says, and if they have nothing else to say, then they'll start an argument just to give their throats some exercise. Daddy always tells that old joke about the three fastest ways to spread news—telegraph, telephone, and tell a woman.

Mama said, "We'll work out something Saturday night." She was quiet for a few seconds then before she said, "All right, I'll meet you down there in a few minutes. My God, you know you can't come up here."

I was about to slip the tennis shoe back on my foot, but it fell right out of my hands. That heavy rubber sole hit the floor like a soft thump on a big bass drum. I stood up right away, pushing out on the screen door, then taking my hand away quick so that the door slammed loud. While the bang was still echoing, I heard the phone receiver being slammed back on the hook.

Mama said, "Who's that?"

"Me. Mark."

"What are you doing home?"

I started up the stairs, walking carefully to keep my weight off the heel. "I stepped on a nail. The doctor said I ought to stay off the foot the rest of the day."

At the top of the stairs the afternoon light came in harsh from the window. Mama looked at me closely, a funny kind of expression on her face.

She said, "Lord, you must have a fever! You're red as fire."

"No. I don't have a fever. I just stepped on a nail."

After a few seconds she said, "Were you standing downstairs there? I thought I heard some kind of noise."

I looked her straight in the eye and lied. "I just dropped my shoe when I opened the door."

She followed me into the kitchen. Sitting down, I pulled the gauze from my heel so she could see how bad it was.

She said, "You had no business out there working. You're too young to be around places where you might get hurt."

"The job didn't hurt me any, Mama. I'm going back tomorrow."

"It's your daddy's fault."

"Look, Mama, it was my fault. I'm the one stepped on the nail!"

"Lord, can't you even see a nail big as a pencil sticking up in a board?"

"There was so much stuff like that around I got careless. I wasn't watching."

"Learn to keep your eyes open, Mark. If you want to take care of yourself you have to keep your eyes open."

"And your ears too, huh, Mama?"

For just an instant that hard kind of wondering expression came over her face again. I looked straight into those pretty green eyes. Then she turned away from me, picking up her purse and car keys.

"I'll go to the store and get some iodine for that foot. Take yourself a bath, honey. I'll be back in a few minutes."

I nodded and she walked out to the hallway. Sitting there, I heard her going down the stairs. The screen door slammed. Then the door of the Plymouth. Then the car started.

I moved to the living room. Out that window I could see the car going down the hill. Mama stopped at the intersection, but she didn't turn. The car crossed the street, heading east toward the fairgrounds parking sections, where normally there wasn't any traffic at all. I was going to watch the car out of sight, but it never got far beyond the fairgrounds. Pretty soon it pulled up under a tree in one of the lots. A person watching from the apartment the way I was couldn't recognize anybody in the car. In fact, it was hard to tell even that there was anybody in it.

I was glad of that. Within two minutes, while I stood there on one foot hating to move and trying to keep from thinking, a brown car that I didn't recognize pulled up beside the black Plymouth. I could see Mama getting out of the Plymouth. Then she walked to the other car. In about a minute it headed off east toward the thick trees this side of the river.

I limped into the bathroom and ran me the deepest tub I could get without the water running out the overflow drain. Then I took off my clothes and sank into the tub. I felt like George Raft in that *Scarface* movie, standing there flipping that half-dollar, waiting for his best friend to shoot him dead. I let my head slip under the water and I waited, holding my breath as long as I could. Then I took a deep breath through my nose. I guess it wasn't too deep though, because as soon as the burning and choking started I came up fast, spitting water. I just don't see how it's possible to commit suicide by drowning unless you jump off a boat in the middle of the Pacific Ocean. And then I'll bet a guy would keep swimming as long at he could, probably wondering why the devil he ever jumped in.

Then I decided that if I really hurried I could pack a bag and get out of the house before Mama got back. I wasn't sure where I was going, but I could go somewhere. Maybe I would just head west to Dallas and find myself a job at that big Centennial show. I didn't have a suitcase. I pulled Daddy's sweet-smelling grip out of the closet and stuffed it with underwear and socks. The odor of that sweet leather filled my nostrils, and I remembered Daddy—with that sweat running into the white undershirt and his glasses getting so wet he could hardly see through them.

I took the socks and underwear out and put the grip back into the closet.

I lay down on the bed. I don't really know how long I had been lying there when Mama came back up the steps and into my room. I was staring at the ceiling.

She sat down on the bed beside me. Her face was as beautiful warm and rosy as I had ever seen it. I tried not to smell the sweetness of her, but I couldn't help it. I wanted to put every thought of her completely out of my mind. I tried to forget her cooking all morning in the hot kitchen or her body bent over a scrub board in the bathtub washing my clothes or her long pretty fingers on the piano keyboard playing some favorites of mine like "My Blue Heaven," "They Cut Down the Old Pine Tree," or "The Isle of Capri."

I rolled over on my stomach while she put the iodine on my heel. She just turned the bottle over the nail hole and held it there for a minute. Then she turned my foot quickly so that no iodine ran down when she took the bottle away.

She said, "Sugar, your face looks so tight. You're not going to cry, are you? I never saw you cry over a hurt before."

"Don't worry. I'm not going to cry."

"Why, back there in the seventh grade that baseball almost knocked your eye out. You didn't cry a bit then. And now you're two years older."

"I wish I wasn't."

"No you don't. You're in so big a hurry to be a man that you can hardly wait."

She turned her head and looked down at the heel again. I felt her hand, cool and fresh, softly covering the nail hole.

She said, "It's all puffed up around that hole. I can feel it throbbing from the pain."

I didn't say anything. She leaned over me and kissed me on the cheek as she stood up. "Go to sleep for a while, honey. After I get your daddy home I'll fix a good supper and wake you up."

"I'm not sleepy."

"All right, I'll play the piano and that'll put you to sleep." Standing by the door, she looked down at me again. "I'll close the door. That way the music won't be too loud."

Lying there, I heard the music, the music that I had been hearing for as long as I could remember, the songs that no matter where I heard them I always connected with my mother's fingers moving over a keyboard.

My heel still hurt, but when I put my mind on the music I didn't notice the pain nearly as much.

EIGHT

I CAME out of the Century Theater about eight o'clock, where I had just seen a new picture with Gary Cooper called *Mr. Deeds Goes to Town*. I thought it was a wonderful picture, even though I hadn't really wanted to see it at first. But it was a choice of Gary Cooper in that or else Shirley Temple in *Little Miss* somebody or another. Not that I had anything against Shirley, it was just that I had outgrown that sort of movie. Now that she was making more money probably than J. P. Morgan there had been a lot of silly talk about her. For example, I remember reading in the paper one day where a British newspaper had said that Shirley wasn't just a little kid but actually a dwarf, thirty years old, and already married to a little person just like her. I certainly didn't believe any such nonsense as that, but I had reached the point where a Shirley Temple picture left me feeling like I had eaten a dozen Milky Ways and Baby Ruths all mixed together in one big bowl.

That Mr. Deeds picture was really fine though. Just because Mr. Deeds didn't care a whole lot about this money he'd inherited, some folks tried to prove he was crazy. The court scene was a real whinger. Gary hadn't wanted to say anything to defend himself, but finally Jean Arthur talked him into getting on the stand. I don't blame Gary for being convinced, because she is really a honey who sort of reminds me of V. Mae Ross in lots of ways. Anyhow, Gary got up there on the stand and started talking about people being pixilated, and pretty soon he had proved that almost everybody is crazy in some way. There was also a fine *March of Time,* all about the fighting during the past six months in Ethiopia. The *March of Time* music is always pretty catchy, and I like the way it ends when that deep-voiced announcer says "Time marches on!"

On that nice Saturday evening I was sort of marching myself during that walk around to the apartment. We still had an hour before the stores closed. Mama had bought me two shirts and two pairs of nice trousers that afternoon, but she and Daddy were supposed to take me to The Emporium around eight o'clock to get a new pair of shoes. It had sure been a nice day. We had finished the job just before two o'clock, and Daddy said he'd cleared about a hundred and twenty dollars. And his fifty-dollar check had come from the VA that morning, so I guess nobody had seen him out there laying those brick. And best of all, no bricklayers had come by the job to call Daddy a scab or a nigger-lover. I sure had hated to say goodbye to old Ward and Roberts and Brewer. I knew I'd see them again, probably plenty of times, but it would never really be as good as that week when I first worked like a real man.

Our car was gone. I went up the dark stairs wondering why the folks hadn't come home yet. They had told me to be sure to get home by eight. The Emporium was only about five blocks from the house, so I wasn't too worried about getting around there in time. But I was still bothered, I don't know why. It was like things had been going too good for a couple of days, and I was afraid it had to end.

The heat had sort of settled in upstairs. I turned on the two fans that Daddy had bought out of the pawnshop that afternoon. I also turned on the radio to hear the Lucky Strike Hit Parade. It made me feel closer to Carl, since I could picture him and John and some of the others sitting around listening up at Wesley. Some of the boys made bets on what the top three songs would be each week.

But the minutes shot by fast, and I was sure worried about

getting those shoes when I finally heard the car pull up downstairs. I was all the way down there before anybody could get out.

It was Daddy by himself. He just sat there, not saying anything.

I said, "Gosh, I was afraid nobody would get here in time. I have to go get those shoes."

When he started talking I knew he had been drinking, even though as dark as it was I couldn't see right away that his hair had come down over his forehead when he put the straw hat on. He said, "Don't worry, Mark, we'll get you some shoes. And I still owe you five dollars for working."

"Just three. You gave me two this afternoon. And we'll just put that three on the shoes. But the store is going to close in about fifteen minutes, and I have to catch the bus at eleven in the morning. Where's Mama?"

"She went off and left me sitting in a damned restaurant. Your mama and some of her fine friends."

"What friends?"

"Some of her women friends and their husbands."

He started getting out of the car. "You wait, Mark. I'm going up and turn the lights out. Then we'll go for a little ride."

"I'll go up and turn the lights out."

"Get in the car and sit down!" Then he softened his voice. "I'm sorry, boy. I didn't mean to yell at you. But I need to go upstairs myself."

Pretty soon the door opened and he came back down the steps, walking pretty steady, the long sleeves of his white shirt turned up a couple of lengths, and the hair pushed back now under his straw hat.

I said, "Daddy, can I drive?"

"You can't drive, boy. All you ever did was steer a car."

"Up at school this spring I drove a tractor quite a bit, when they used it to cut wood. A Negro man named Sam always let me drive it to the shed when they finished."

"That's not the same thing. You might could make the car go

all right, but you have to have sense to handle it in traffic. Especially this Saturday night traffic in Jackson. Half the people on the streets are drunk."

"Yes sir."

He drove out into North State. We passed the Old Capitol and moved along South State.

He said, "Maybe you think I'm drunk, Mark. Is that it?"

"No sir, I don't think you're drunk."

"I'm not. There's enough on my mind to keep me sober no matter how much I drink."

"How come, Daddy? Are the union bricklayers going to jump on you or something?"

He glanced at me and laughed, his lips widening to show those fine false teeth he was so proud of. "Damn the union. They ain't about to jump on me. Fifty-eight years old, and I can whip hell out of the whole bunch."

"I don't know, Daddy. Some of them look pretty tough."

"It's not how tough they look, it's how tough they are. Don't let anybody's looks ever scare you. That's a thing you have to learn. Maybe you forget Kid McCoy told me that night in Memphis that I could have been a big-time middleweight?"

"No sir, I sure wouldn't forget that."

That night in Memphis was back on April 22, 1896. Daddy still had that yellowed clipping stuck in an old tin box along with a lot of pictures and papers from the army days in France. He even had a lock of his mother's own hair in that box. I had prowled in there several times, and I remember the tinny mothball smell and the strange feeling I got holding that strand of hair. That old newspaper clipping told a great deal about Kid McCoy knocking out Frank Bosworth in the second round. But it also said at the bottom of the column that Carl Torrance had beaten Skippy Malone in four rounds. There weren't any details about Daddy's fight, but he had told Carl and me several times that Malone was an experienced fighter, supposed to be on the way up, and Daddy was just an eighteen-year-old kid. I never asked him about any of his other fights. It all seemed as far back in time as Moses leading the Israelites through the Red Sea.

We pulled up in front of the State Cafe. I started to get out of the car. He told me not to. He didn't stay but a minute in there, and then we were moving down the street to another cafe. He still wouldn't let me get out. But he was back right away.

We stopped at Marty's, down at the end of South State. I sat in the car watching Daddy talk to a man behind the counter. The man shook his head a couple of times, but Daddy didn't seem to be arguing with him or anything like that. There was a neon sign behind the window, and a lot of bugs buzzed and fluttered as though they could reach that light by going through the glass. There were hundreds of them, darting and zinging, plenty of them smashing themselves against the glass.

After a minute or two Daddy came out of Marty's and got back in the car. His brow was all wrinkled up. That reminded me how he was always telling me not to frown that way. He'd say, "You'll look like you're forty years old before you get to be twenty."

I said, "What's the matter, Daddy?"

Suddenly he doubled up his right fist and just pounded the top of the steering wheel about three times in a row. "God-dam!" He practically shouted it. I looked around fast, hoping there wasn't a policeman or even other people in those cars parked there. But I didn't see anybody.

I put my hand on his shoulder and leaned close to him. I could smell the whiskey smell mixed with the odor of that sun-browned skin, the smell like that of a man. When I touched his arm he pulled away very suddenly.

"Get back there!"

"Please, Daddy, let's go home."

He looked at me like he wanted to cry. "It's all right, Mark. I wasn't pushing you away from me. You know I think the world of my boys."

He started pulling at his shirt tail, and I couldn't figure what he was doing. The shirt had been kind of rumpled up above his belt, but I didn't want to tell him to tuck it in. From under his shirt he pulled out his hand and I saw that the fans weren't the only things he got out of the pawnshop. He was holding that black forty-five pistol.

"That damned thing weighs a ton," he said. "Jammed against my guts that way it's a wonder it didn't fall and blow my toes off."

"You said it had a safety so that it wouldn't go off unless it was being squeezed by a hand."

"That's right, boy. You remembered that. I thought you forgot."

I remembered almost everything he'd told me almost three years before, just before he put the pistol in the pawnshop for that long rest. I remember he said that I was never to touch it except in an emergency, when no one else was around and I needed it to save myself. He let me hold it that day, and I remember the heavy weight, almost too much for my arm when I tried to extend it. Maybe I could hold it now that I was bigger, especially since I'd been handling those bricks all week.

"Why did you bring the pistol, Daddy?"

"I thought I might get a chance to see how a man looks on the other end of it."

"You told me to never point it at anything I didn't intend to kill."

"That's right, Mark. That's another good rule you ought never to forget."

The blunt-nosed thing was lying on the seat between us, like some kind of Satan machine that might have a mind of its own and any minute turn on me and blow my insides out.

"Daddy, do something with it. Put it away, please."

"Don't worry, Mark. Things will be all right now. I'm not thinking about pointing it at anything now. I need a drink. You're going to cross the river with me and I'll have a drink. Then we'll go home and go to bed."

He slid the pistol under the car seat. We drove toward the

Pearl River bridge, only a couple of blocks away, and started across. A steady stream of traffic hit us hard in the face with their headlights. The bridge was so narrow that I thought the car was going to scrape the concrete railing. But Daddy didn't wobble the wheel too much, and I guess he did a better job than I could have done. For almost a mile after we crossed the bridge the road wound along beside the river. Off in the water I could hear the croaking of the frogs and smell the hot dampness and mud stink. Our headlights seemed to be moving into a million bugs. At least half of them must have smashed themselves against our windshield.

Daddy pulled under a pine tree at a place called Shady Rest. Three or four cars were parked there, but nobody was in them. He wanted to go inside, but I asked him to please stay out there and have his drink in the car. When he saw how worried I was, he put his hand on the back of my neck. I could feel the hard calluses.

He said, "Don't worry about a thing, boy."

A Negro came out to the car. Daddy ordered a pint of Four Roses and a Coke. While he waited for the bottle, Daddy said, "I want you to go back to that school and win that speaking medal, you hear? I'm going to be proud of you."

"Don't worry. I'll win all right. I've practiced so much that I deserve to win."

"Are the other boys any good?"

"They're all right, but they don't really care a lot about it. They never practice much at all."

That was sure the truth. Warren Anderson hadn't even learned his declamation completely by the time I left there, and Allison McGee was in the contest only because Miss McKinley had promised him some extra points in English. She was the speaking coach, and she said there ought to be at least three people in it to have any kind of contest.

The Negro brought the whiskey and Coke out to the car. Daddy gave him a five-dollar bill. While the Negro was fishing around for the change, Daddy looked at the Coke. He held the bottle up to the light coming from the tops of two posts in the parking lot.

"All right," Daddy said. "What am I supposed to do—bite the damned top off the Coke?"

The Negro said, "No sir, Captain. No, sir-ree, you sure don't need to do that. I didn't understand you was going to drink right here. I'd be happy to bring you a glass with some ice."

"What I want is the goddam top off the bottle. In a hurry."

"Yes sir, Captain." He grabbed the bottle and ran back inside the Shady Rest.

"Don't jump on him, Daddy. Don't make him feel bad."

"I didn't jump on him."

The Negro came back out with the bottle and gave Daddy his change.

Daddy said, "Here, boy. Here's fifty cents so you won't forget to pop the top off my Coke next time."

The Negro grinned and bowed. "No sir, Captain. You know I won't ever forget that anymore. You sure you wouldn't like a glass and a little ice?"

"To hell with that. I'm a bottle baby."

Laughing and slapping his hands together, the Negro went on back to the Shady Rest. Daddy opened the whiskey bottle. Then he turned the bottle up, and I winced a little bit as the liquor gurgled down his throat. I tried not to think what that much whiskey would do to his stomach. The evangelist John Gabriel had said that the heat from even a small drink was enough to fry an egg. My daddy just didn't take any small drinks.

When he put the bottle down, he shuddered a little and made a loud tearing cough before he got the Coke up to his mouth. He took a short drink of that. Then he leaned back against the seat, holding the two bottles on his lap. His big neck broadened when he relaxed back on the seat. The light from those two posts in the parking lot shone faintly on his face.

I didn't want him to go to sleep. After a minute I said, "Are you ready to go home now, Daddy?"

He didn't open his eyes when he answered. "Not just yet, boy. I'll rest here a minute, huh? That all right with you?"

"Sure, but you can go home and have a nice bed to stretch out in."

"A nice bed all to myself."

"Mama will be home when we get there. You wait and see. She'll be sitting there wondering where we've been."

He opened his eyes and looked at me. "I hope I live long enough that someday we can sit and have a drink together, Mark. You and me and your brother."

"You'll have to live a long time, Daddy. I'm never going to drink any of that stuff."

"I hope you don't. But if you do, someday we might have one together."

His head was resting on the back of the seat, his eyes sort of staring at the entrance of the Shady Rest. After a minute he said, "Shady Rest, Shady Rest. That's a helluva name for a bootleg joint. Sounds like a damned cemetery. I guess, by God, it ain't far from one at that. Shady Rest. Jesus Christ."

"Please don't talk like that."

"Don't convert me, Mark. Not tonight, huh?"

"The Lord will not hold him guiltless that taketh His name in vain."

"No reason why He should. You're a good boy, Mark."

He was breathing very relaxed now, his big chest pulling in long and easy at the damp night air. I was afraid he was getting sleepy again, but his eyes were still open, seeming to look through the bug-spattered windshield at something that was far off out in the night.

Finally he said, "It ain't much, is it, boy? Not too much at that, is it?"

"What, Daddy?"

"Just a chance to sit in the woods a few minutes and have a

drink. A man don't have much to look forward to, but at least he's got that."

"You've got more than that, Daddy."

"Sure, I don't mean it the way you think. I've got my boys—you and Carl."

"And Mama."

"I'm getting old, Mark. I'm fifty-eight. Your mama is still a young woman."

"You don't look old."

"Yeah, but a man can't kid himself."

Then I just couldn't help myself. I said, "Daddy, don't you believe in Jesus Christ?"

"When you get older you'll wish you hadn't asked me that."

"But do you believe? Because that's all you need. 'Believe on the Lord Jesus Christ and thou shalt be saved.' That's what the Bible says."

"No, Mark, I don't think it's that easy. I've started scabbing here on earth, but I don't think I can scab my way to Heaven. A man's got to have a paid-up card for that."

"Daddy, the thief on the cross changed his mind at the last minute. And Christ said that the man would that day be with Him in Paradise."

He took another swig from the Four Roses bottle. This time he didn't drink much Coke at all. He said, "That's a fine idea you got there, boy. What do you think I am, some kind of cheap bastard that don't believe in paying his own way? You can't ask a man to go to Heaven that way."

"There is a multitude of rejoicing in Heaven at the conversion of a real first-class sinner."

"Like fishing, you mean? They catch a whopper and it makes them real happy, huh?"

"Don't make a joke out of it, Daddy."

He held the bottles in one hand and he reached over and caught my left hand. "I'm sorry, Mark. You know I wouldn't make fun of you. I belong to the Methodist church. You know that, don't you?"

"Yes sir, but I don't think I ever saw you go to church at all."

"That don't mean I forgot everything I believed. When I was a young boy about your age, I remember one day after church up in Memphis. I leaned against a tree and looked right up in the sky and I knew God was there. I knew it then. But things—hell, I don't know, boy. Something happens to a man, most men—makes them forget. A man gets afraid it's all nothing."

" 'Purge me with hyssop and I shall be clean. Wash me and I shall be whiter than snow.' Psalms fifty-one, seven."

He turned to me. "Hyssop. What's hyssop?"

"I don't really know. Some kind of plant they had back in King David's time."

A few people had come and gone, but there were still three cars besides ours at the Shady Rest. Daddy was so relaxed and talking so soft and easy that I didn't really care if we spent the rest of the night sitting right there. A few mosquitoes zinged down on us, but he lit a Roi Tan cigar and the thick, good-smelling smoke helped drive them away.

When the four men came out and stood on the little steps I didn't recognize them at first, but Daddy's body went hard and straight, like a cat going all stiff-haired at the bark of a dog that was still locked in a yard.

Then I recognized them. I said, "Start the car, Daddy. Start the car and back up a little. Then you can swing around right into the road."

He didn't move, but just stared at them. The four of them stood no less than twenty yards from us—Bud Stout, Corley Webb, that dark guy Shaw, and another one I didn't know.

"Back off, Daddy. Back off and turn around."

His voice was quiet, but the happy, relaxed tone was gone. "No, Mark, we won't back off. I appreciate all you've been telling me about God, but I'm telling you something about men. The first thing is not to back off. Don't ever back off from a goddam man."

"But there's four of them, Daddy. And only two of us."

He reached down onto the floor boards of the car. "You counted wrong. There's three of us."

He sat still, not trying to attract their attention, but he put the top on the Four Roses bottle. Then he held the pistol in his right hand down on the seat.

Corley Webb pointed his finger at the car. Then all four of them looked our way, shading their eyes against the glare from those lights on top of the posts.

Bud stout walked about halfway to us and stopped. "That you out there, Carl?"

Daddy said, nice and easy, "Yeah, Bud, this is Carl."

"I'd like to talk to you, Carl."

"You can talk to me, Bud. You and Corley. Damn the other two."

The other three walked up to where Bud was, and then the four of them came toward the car together.

Daddy shifted the pistol over to his left hand, holding it against the car door and his leg, so that the men standing outside couldn't have seen it. Bud and Corley came and stood right outside the car door. Shaw and the other man stood behind them.

Corley said, "Ain't seen you all week, Carl. Where you keeping yourself?"

Daddy said, "Don't bullshit me, Corley."

Even in that bad light you could see the beet-redness of Bud Stout's face. I guess he wasn't really a bad guy, but Mama was right when she said it would take two cases of beer to fill Bud up.

Bud said, "Carl, me and Corley wish you hadn't done this to us. We've always been your friends."

"I know that, Bud. I've just been doing what I had to do."

Bud leaned closer to the car door. I was afraid if he got any closer he would see the pistol. He said, "You got to understand us, Carl. You ought to come and talked to us if you just had to have money."

Daddy puffed some cigar smoke. "Talk, talk—that's all the hell I've heard since I came back from Memphis. Union talk don't put clothes on my kids or pay their school bills."

That big dark guy Shaw pushed his way between Bud and Corley. He said, "I'm Al Shaw, Mr. Torrance. I'd like to meet you."

Daddy said, "Don't bullshit me, Shaw. We met."

"Yeah, but I didn't take a real good look at you then. I want to see you up close. I never had a real good look at a scabbing nigger-loving bastard."

The words sort of hung in the air, and even sitting close to that door the way he was, Daddy punched so fast he seemed to meet the words halfway. Daddy bought Carl and me a punching bag a couple of years ago, one of those fast-striking kind. He hung it on the ceiling of the back porch, and Carl and I stood on a chair to hit it. Daddy showed us how to punch it, but we never got as fast as he was with it. Daddy could put both fists together and hardly seeming to move his hands over three inches each time he could make that bag slam like thunder against the top of the porch, as fast as old Camonte's machine guns in *Scarface*.

So even though he didn't move his left arm much at all, his fist caught Shaw as he leaned forward, getting ready to say something else. Shaw wobbled back, holding his nose and cussing all the time. Opening the car door with his left hand, Daddy handed me the gun with his right. He spoke very soft. "Use it if you have to, boy. Don't let but one jump me at a time."

He moved out that door fast, so surprising fast for the short heavyset man he was, like he was laying a string of brick that his life depended on. He didn't spar around, none of that John L. Sullivan pose or stuff that some fighters try to use. He tucked his chin under his left shoulder and piled into Shaw like a hungry bulldog into a chunk of raw meat. As tall as Shaw was, he backed off and stuck out his arms, but Daddy threw punches into his belly from a crouch. When Shaw dropped his arms to cover his stomach, Daddy's fists flew into his face, like an axe cutting into a soft-wooded tree.

Shaw went down. Daddy didn't wait for him to get up, but

fell on top of him, still punching while Shaw rolled and tried to shake him off.

I was trembling all over. I stuck that big pistol in my back pocket, what part of it would go there, and I came out of the car, feeling the weight of it tugging at the seat of my pants.

Bud said, "Hell, Corley, let's break this thing up."

Corley didn't have time to answer. The blond-headed man that I didn't know said, "You men keep away. I'll fix that scab."

He moved almost as fast as Daddy moved earlier. I should have had that pistol out, keeping him off, but I didn't. Just as Daddy drew his right arm back to really land one on Shaw, the blond-headed man threw his right knee hard into the side of Daddy's face. Not expecting it at all, Daddy sagged and rolled off Shaw. The blond-headed man jumped on top of Daddy. All in a few seconds, it seemed, there was Daddy getting the worst of it. The man was holding Daddy's right arm down with his left knee, and he was punching hard and fast into Daddy's face. Daddy tried to roll his head with the punches. He rolled to the right side. I was close and he was looking right at me. He didn't say a word—just looked at me.

I didn't try to think at all anymore. I had the pistol out of my back pocket before anybody knew what was happening. I swung the pistol around like a man throwing the discus and slammed it as hard as I could against the side of that blond bastard's head.

The way he rolled over I might as well have shot him. I threw the pistol at Bud's feet and jumped on that blond bastard's back. I locked my legs around his belly like Yaqui Joe getting a scissors on Dutch Mandell down at the wrestling matches. I put my left arm around his neck and started punching with my right fist. I was fighting that man and that guy Shaw and Will Tarzun and everybody I had ever in my life been afraid of. As long as I kept punching, it was the best feeling I ever had.

NINE

THERE WAS a stop sign where the dirt road from the Shady Rest ran into US 80. I hated to stop, because I'd had so much trouble finally getting away from that bootleg place that I was afraid I wouldn't be able to get the car moving again. I don't really know exactly how we did get away from there. All I remember is Bud Stout pulling me off that blond-headed man, Shaw lying there on the ground howling and cussing, and finally me and Daddy in the front seat with Bud and Corley slamming the doors and pointing toward the road.

The only thing was that I was on the driver's side.

Bud said, "Get the car going, Mark. Get it the hell out of here."

I looked at Daddy. His head was back against the seat, seeming to be relaxed about the way he was before the whole mess started. The difference was that now his left eye and cheek bone were all swollen and bloody, and he just sat there like he was a million miles away from everything.

I had pressed my toes against the starter with my heel against the accelerator, the same way I'd seen Daddy and Mama do hundreds of times. But after the motor started, I shifted the gear and let out the clutch so fast that the car bucked like somebody had slammed it from behind. Bucked and stopped. I started the motor again. I let out the clutch. It jerked so hard to a stop this time that Daddy even opened his eyes and looked over at me.

Bud stuck his head in the window. "Christ, boy, can't you drive?"

"Sure. Sure I can drive. It's just that I have trouble starting."

"You let the clutch out too fast. Take it easy."

That time I did it, and I was amazed when the car started to roll. I shifted on into second as fast as I could and finally into high to get away from that jerkiness.

The half-mile or so of dirt road wasn't any trouble because I didn't meet any traffic coming the other way at all. But now there was that big yellow stop sign grinning at me like a Halloween mask, grinning and sneering in my headlights. I was going to run on past it, even if it was breaking the law, but traffic was coming at me on that concrete highway and I had to stop the car. The car was at the top of an incline, and I knew what was going to happen.

You see, I forgot to shift to neutral or to use the clutch at the stop. The car just conked out again and started slipping backward down the hill. I put my right foot on the brake and my left on the clutch. I reached my toes from the brake over to the starter again. The motor caught on, and I moved real fast to the gas pedal. I tried to give it the gas and let a little clutch out and hold it on the hill that way. But I just couldn't balance it out.

When the motor died and we started rolling back, the sweat was also rolling off my face. My hand trembled as I shifted that gear stick again. Behind me in the mirror I could see two other cars' headlights moving up the road behind me.

Daddy opened his eyes and looked at me. "You just can't drive it, can you, boy?"

"Daddy, I'm trying. But I'm nervous and scared."

"You knocked a man off my back. You took a pistol and knocked him off my back."

"Yes, I did."

"Then stop acting like a baby now. Pull up that emergency

brake. That'll hold the bastard. Give a lot of gas and let out so slow on the clutch that you think you're not letting out at all. When you get moving take that emergency brake off."

"Can't you see good enough to do the driving?"

"Yeah, I can. But I want you to do it."

The cars behind me started honking. I didn't know whether to be glad or sorry. At least it wasn't Shaw and his friend. I don't think they'd have been sitting there honking at us.

Daddy started to stick his head out the window. I said, "Please, Daddy, please! Don't yell anything at them back there."

The highway was clear and this time I let the clutch out slow—so slow, like Daddy said, that it was almost like I wasn't letting it out at all. The old Plymouth caught the power, I threw off the emergency brake, and even though I spun a little dirt with my back wheels I made it onto the highway heading back to Jackson.

I didn't drive too fast, and there wasn't much to it as long as the car was moving. I had steered lots of times. But when we came to the bridge I got nervous again because that thing is so narrow. I met two cars coming the other way, and each time I hugged my side of the bridge, holding my breath for fear we'd scrape the side.

By the time we got to the house, I was even good enough to stop without killing the motor. I looked toward the upstairs apartment. The lights were burning.

I held Daddy's arm when we went upstairs, but he was really moving pretty well by himself. He hadn't said much though. The forty-five was hanging about halfway out of my back pocket, but I told myself that even if it fell out it couldn't go off because nobody was squeezing the grip. When I opened the door to the big bedroom-living room, there was Mama dressed in her pink kimono, sipping a cup of coffee.

She said, "Well, if you're not a sight, Carl. You just about take the prize for the biggest mess I ever saw."

Daddy stood by the door looking at her, not saying a word.

I said, "He might be hurt bad, Mama. Look at his eye."

Mama said, "I wonder what the VA will give you for that, Carl. Go up there Monday morning and tell them you can't see a thing out of it."

Daddy said, "Where's your boyfriend? Under the goddam bed?"

Her face flamed bright red. "What's wrong with you, Carl, for God's sake? What kind of talk is that in front of Mark?"

"Honest talk, Clara. I want to hear some honest talk for a change."

Mama went into the kitchen. She took a washcloth and wrung it in cool water from the faucet. Without looking around, she said, "You've been looking for trouble all evening. I see you finally found it. Who beat you up?"

Daddy sat on the sofa. "Beat me up? That's a goddam joke. Ask Mark here if that ain't a goddam joke."

Mama came back with the wet rag. "Take that shirt off before you get blood and filth all over the couch. Then sit back down."

Daddy stood up. I helped him take his shirt off.

Mama said, "Who was it? Who'd you fight with?"

"Not the one I was looking for. But I guess you know that—since you probably just left him."

Mama threw the washrag in his face. "Take it, take it and clean your own filthy face! It's too bad you can't wipe off your dirty heart and make it clean too!"

Daddy came springing off that sofa the same way he'd jumped from the car earlier to punch Shaw. He doubled his fists and moved three steps to Mama before I could even think.

He said, "You don't throw anything in my face, by Jesus! I'll break your neck!"

He had actually drawn his fist back, but by that time I was between them, throwing myself around Daddy's arms. "Please, Daddy, sit down! Please."

He tried to brush me away, but he didn't try very hard.

Mama looked as though she'd turned to ice right on the spot. She said, "Leave him alone, Mark. Get out of his way. Let him show you the kind of man he really is."

With the veins of his neck all bulged out and his arms and legs tight with the strain, Daddy looked like one of those statues at the Old Capitol dedicated to the dead of the World War. For the longest time they just stood there staring, almost like they were daring each other to make the first move. It reminded me of two boys mad at each other but neither one wanting to throw the first lick, the kind who stand and glare at each other and no matter how much the other boys try to egg them on, the two boys do nothing.

Finally Daddy settled back on his heels and relaxed. He even smiled. "It's all right. We'll talk about this after Mark goes to sleep."

Mama said, "You might as well talk in front of him now. He knows now what you think of me."

"Just let it go right now, Clara. We'll talk about it later."

"I won't be here later. I'm packing my clothes and leaving. Thank God that Mark and Carl Junior have a place they can go to school and live. A good Christian place where they can get away from your influence."

"Oh, yes, you're the holy one, huh?"

Mama picked up the washrag and went back into the kitchen. She wet the rag again. I followed her in there.

I said, "Mama, don't go anywhere. Don't leave Daddy."

"You get ready for bed, Mark. It's midnight and you need some rest. You've worked like a slave on that job all week and you have to catch that bus in the morning."

She pulled an ice cube from the refrigerator tray and wrapped the washcloth around it. She walked back to the living room and gave the cloth to Daddy, who was sitting down again. She said, "Put it on your eye, Carl. It's too late for anything to keep it from turning black, but it might help some."

Daddy took the rag and nodded his head. They looked into

each other's eyes for several seconds. Then Mama turned away all at once and looked back at me. "Get your clothes off and get in bed, Mark. You've heard all you're going to hear tonight."

That heavy forty-five was still sagging the seat of my trousers. I said, "Here's the pistol, Daddy."

Daddy grabbed that pistol like he'd found a long-lost friend. He held it in his lap with one hand and the rag on his eye with the other. He said, "Well, I got one thing for myself out of that week's work. I got something I can walk the streets and feel like a man with."

Mama said, "You got something you can walk the streets with and get yourself arrested." She stood in front of him and stuck out her hand.

Daddy said, "What in hell's wrong with you?"

"You've got no business with a thing like that in the house. You don't have enough responsibility. Give it to me."

"Oh, Clara, you watch me from now on. You'll see how much responsibility I have."

Mama stayed right in front of him. She didn't reach for the pistol, but simply held out her hand. "I want the pistol, Carl. A man who drinks can't be trusted with a pistol. Give me the miserable thing!"

Daddy held the pistol, looking down at it with a kind of respect and tenderness on his face. He shook his head slowly. Then he seemed to sigh and handed the pistol to her.

Right away she dropped the bullet clip out. Then she slid the mechanism back and forth a couple of times to be sure that she hadn't left a single bullet in there. Mama knew how to handle a pistol. Then she gave it back to Daddy.

"You can put it up somewhere now, Carl." She spoke as if she were telling a child to be careful with his toys.

"I don't want the bastard now. You know I don't even have another cartridge left."

"I know that."

"Then what do I want with that damned thing?"

"You put it in one of your drawers and leave it there. If you ever think there's a burglar coming up those stairs you tell me and I'll give you the bullet clip."

Then she turned to me. "Mark, if I have to tell you one more time to get in bed I'm going to scream so loud that brass eagle on the New Capitol will take off flying!"

Daddy said, "Don't yell at that boy. He stayed by me like a man tonight."

Mama said, "Yes, and you got drunk and we didn't get him any shoes."

I said, "Don't worry about that, Mama."

"Go to bed, Mark!"

I went into the bedroom and took off my clothes. I could faintly hear them talking, sometimes their voices getting a little loud but not loud enough I could tell what they were saying. I lay down on the bed. My body felt something was sitting on my shoulders while my feet and legs were being pulled under in quicksand.

In a few minutes I heard Daddy splashing in the tub. I was so tired I wanted to close my eyes and never open them again, but I couldn't go to sleep. Thinking about all that had happened, I trembled a little, remembering the way I'd hit that man.

Then I started to really wonder about Mama and Daddy. At first, it had been hard to think about that day Mama had been on the telephone. It was like a bad disease that I knew might hit a lot of people, but never me. I remembered what she'd said about some of the small kids from broken homes up at Wesley. I wasn't a small kid anymore, but I didn't want to be from a broken home. No matter how mad Mama and Daddy got at each other, I just didn't see how they could be happy if they weren't together. In three more years I'd be through with high school and maybe in college or a CCC somewhere. But it hurt to think they wouldn't have each other.

I had blamed Mama a lot at first. But the more I thought about it the more I just felt sad about the whole thing, not blaming anybody especially. Sure, it was a sickening thing that Mama had gone to see another man, just sickening and shameful. But I had been thinking about old King Solomon and David, two people that had actually talked with God and who were still, at times, mighty wicked. I had never understood how a man could actually talk with God one day and then the next be plotting to have Bathsheba's husband killed the way David did. I mean, he actually had her husband killed so he could have that woman. It sure makes a person wonder.

But then I think about myself, how I spent those hours in study hall looking at V. Mae's legs, how I enjoyed the looks of people like Ginger Rogers and Norma Shearer and Alice Faye in the movies, and finally the almost unstoppable feeling I had the day I was looking at that pretty nakedness of Geraldine. I know that if I ever see Geraldine all by herself again there's no telling what might happen, especially if she's feeling the way she was last time. There was a lot I didn't understand about a lot of things in the world. That shows how you can be a straight-A, exempt-from-exams student— and still not know much at all.

I couldn't *think* my way through it at all anymore. I just knew how I *felt*. I sure as the devil didn't hate Mama or anything like that. In fact, I didn't love her one bit less. It's funny. Maybe I even loved her more, knowing how miserable she must have been feeling to let herself fall prey to a situation like that.

I started saying *Lord, Lord, Lord* to myself. And that got me to saying my prayers, trying to talk to God while the fan in the room kept humming away.

That hum had about put me to sleep when a crack of light shot across my face as the door opened. Daddy came close to the bed. I could make out that he had on his old red bathrobe, and I caught the smell of it, the shaving lotion smell and the man smell of my daddy.

He whispered, "Are you asleep, boy?"

"No sir. Not yet."

"You ought to be."

"It's okay. The bus won't leave until eleven. And there won't be anything to do on it but sleep anyway." I hated to think of the boring bus ride, but I was afraid to ask him to let me hitchhike.

He picked up my left hand, wrapping it in both of his. I could feel the calluses in the palms and the smooth tips of his fingers that never got roughened up no matter how many bricks he laid. He always said that by the time he got to be sixty he wouldn't have enough skin on his fingertips to make one good fingerprint. I could see the dark swelling around his cheek and eye. In my mind I called that blond-headed man another bastard. I knew I should have been praying for him instead, but I couldn't bring myself to do that right then.

Like he could read my mind, Daddy said, "Was this the hand you hit him with—the left?"

"Aw, Daddy, I hit him with the pistol. You know that. I couldn't hurt that big man with my fist."

"Which arm did you swing?"

"The pistol was in my right hand."

"That's good. Always use the right when you want to throw everything you've got."

"You make me sound pretty tough, Daddy. But I was so scared I almost didn't know what I was doing."

I remembered the way I had been quoting the Beatitudes with Lance Godbold. *Blessed are the peacemakers: for they shall be called the children of God.* Then I tried to balance out my uneasy feeling with the thought that Christ had fought the money changers and driven them out of the temple.

"You didn't get any new shoes to wear to the speaking, did you?"

"No sir. But it won't matter."

"You can take my shoes."

"I can't do that, Daddy."

Late last summer at a bargain sale he had bought a creamy tan pair at Thom McAn's—really fine-looking shoes that had little holes punched in them for coolness. Daddy hadn't worn them but a couple of weeks then, thinking he would save them for the following summer. I remembered how he polished them very carefully with that neutral polish before he put them away.

He said, "You'll take my shoes and wear them, keep them. When you get on that stage I don't want any of those little snots with a little more money looking better than you."

"But you've hardly worn those shoes at all."

"The damned things are too big for me. But they'll fit you fine. If as much of you grows on top as what you got turned under, you'll be a big man."

"All right, Daddy. I'll take the shoes. Thanks."

"You fought like a man. If I died tomorrow I'd be happy knowing that you and your brother are men and can take care of yourselves."

Then for a couple of minutes he didn't say anything, just held my hand. He squeezed the hand and then took my fingers and rolled them into a fist.

I said, "What is it, Daddy?"

"What?"

"Don't you want to tell me something else?"

Finally he said, "Look, Mark, I was drinking a lot tonight."

"Yes sir."

"I talked a lot too. Said too much. You understand me?"

"About Mama?"

He started talking soft and fast then, saying there were things about a man and woman I didn't understand yet. There were especially things between a husband and wife that could hardly even be guessed at by a boy my age.

He said, "You heard me say something bad about your mama right in there where you were standing. That's about the dirtiest thing I could have done. She ought to shot me with that damned pistol. But, you listen. You don't think any less of your mama because of what I said, you hear me?"

"Yes sir. Is Mama going to leave?"

"No. Hell, no. Nobody's going anywhere. You just forget what I said when I was drinking. You've got the best mama in the world."

Then he squeezed my hand again, and I was afraid at first

that he wasn't going to kiss my cheek the way he used to, but he did. We had shook hands that day in the pool hall when I came in from Wesley, so he really hadn't kissed me since back there in January when Carl and I caught the bus to go back to Wesley from Memphis. One day, before too long, I would probably be so big that it wouldn't seem right for him to ever kiss my cheek again. But I didn't want to rush that time.

"Get your sleep," he said. "You've got to travel tomorrow—in a fine pair of shoes."

"Good night, Daddy."

I knew Mama would be in, but I said good night to the world and waited and she still hadn't come in. Then it seemed I was about to go to sleep. Maybe I did go to sleep, because when I was awake again I realized that Mama was there.

I didn't say anything. Her arm was across my chest, and she had her face down on the pillow with her cheek against mine. I could feel the softness of her pressing against me, and I smelled the face lotion she always put on at night.

I thought she had just kissed me and that had woke me up. But maybe I just thought she kissed me. I didn't open my eyes, but I sort of moaned and mumbled a little. Right away she kissed my forehead and moved away, probably thinking I was waking up. She stood up and then I heard her slippers shuffling out of the room. When I rolled my face around to where she'd had her eyes against the pillow case, I could feel the wetness.

TEN

WHEN I THINK of all the things that happened on my hitch-hiking trip, it sure makes that safe, respectable Tri-State bus seem the dullest ride in the world. The darned bus stopped every time somebody along the road waved a hand, and it was so crowded that I could smell the people on there. A kind of dirty looking old man sat beside me. I didn't have that against him, but he had what Daddy calls the "whiskey sneezes." He'd get started sneezing and he'd really spray the place so bad that you could smell the liquor. I had part of the Sunday Jackson *Daily News* with me, so I just rocked back in the seat and put the newspaper over my face, pretending that I was sleeping. That way I didn't have to breathe so many of those microbes.

I was so bored that I even wished Dudley Belker and Will Tarzun were on the bus. They would probably have been trying to make time with two old lady passengers up front, one of which kept talking about her grandson in the CCC down in Louisiana. To hear her tell it, you'd have thought he was in Ethiopia fighting the Italians instead of swatting mosquitoes down in the swamps.

The whole trip was so bad that I must have said my declamation to myself about twenty times. I went over and over it in my mind, even seeing myself on the stage practicing the gestures and all. I had it down so perfect that it was going to be foolish to even have a contest tomorrow. I hoped that at least Allison and Warren would have learned their speeches by then. I didn't want it to look like I had no competition at all.

The last few miles before we got to the McCool-Wesley road, I took my grip out of the rack and moved up and stood by the door so I could watch for the stop. The driver kind of snarled that he knew where it was, but I wanted to be sure. Floyd Rollins didn't run the mail on Sundays, so unless I was very lucky and caught somebody else I was going to have an eight-mile walk from State 12 to Wesley. I sure didn't want to add a mile and a half to that by going all the way into McCool before I got off the bus.

When we passed the little dirt road outside of Ethel, the one where Mr. Godbold had his shack, I felt pretty bad. Funny, a few days ago I had laughed inside myself at the doctor saying the baby didn't have a chance. I knew then that God could help that little Godbold baby if He really wanted to, but now I didn't know at all, not really. I had just sort of taken for granted that the baby was dead, even though I would still keep praying until I knew for sure. Probably Lance Godbold and his wife had moved on somewhere else, the way the doctor said they would after the baby died.

Still, when we went past that road I looked at it so hard that the bus driver caught my eye in the mirror and shook his head: "That ain't it. You got seven miles yet." I nodded my head and didn't say anything. But I was remembering that even though I had prayed for that little baby during the past week I hadn't really kept thinking and hoping for him the way I should have. Unless a person is a downright hypocrite, when he really cares about somebody's problem he ought to keep that problem on his mind a good bit, not just say a few words in prayer one night and then forget it till the next time. It hurt to think that the little baby was dead. So many other people were living.

When I saw the turn-off to the Wesley road up ahead, I started to reach over and touch the driver's shoulder to let him know. But he was already looking at me in the mirror and nodding his head. After that big gray-and-blue bus roared off toward McCool I stood for a minute trying to let that red dust settle before I had to breathe. Then I picked up Daddy's grip and started walking. I was wearing a pair of tennis shoes because I had figured I might have some hiking to do, and I sure didn't want to get those fine creamy-tan shoes of Daddy's all dusty. I'll bet I couldn't have walked a mile in those fine shoes before that dust would have clogged up all those little breathing holes.

It was very quiet while I crossed that long dusty stretch between the cotton fields. Then I got into the hills with their green pines and red banks, and the road was hard-packed clay in most places so that my feet didn't spank up too much dust. Not a soul came past me going either way. On Sundays most of these folks either go to church or else sit around meditating—sometimes both, but they sure don't do much driving.

It was almost six o'clock and the shadows from the pines were getting long across the road when I finally stood by that gray tin mailbox again. The flag was down. Floyd wouldn't be making any run tonight. I looked up at the white house. Not a sign of a car or people either. The only sounds were a pig grunting and squealing and now and then a chicken cackling or clucking out by the barn.

I looked and looked at the house, afraid in a way to go up there, and yet in another way knowing I would be mad at myself later if I didn't have the guts to try to see her at least one more time.

The door opened and Geraldine came out on the front porch. She wore a white skirt with some kind of white blouse with red flowers printed bright on it.

She said, "Don't just stand there, dummy. Come on up here."

One thing about her, she sure never wastes any words. I walked up to the house and stood at the foot of the steps.

She said, "I've chewed a fingernail off waiting for you."

"I didn't think you'd even remember."

"I'd ask you in the house but I guess I better not."

"Where's your folks?"

"It'll be a while before they come back."

I supposed they had gone to some church services. There was always an evangelist or two holding revivals around Kosciusko. Remembering what Geraldine had said about her papa being so hard on her, I was surprised he hadn't made her go with them.

She said, "You go on over and sit in the grove. Our place." She smiled that clean-toothed smile of hers. "Should I get the Monopoly set?"

"I guess not. I don't really want to play Monopoly, do you?"

"No."

She went back in the house and I walked over to the clump of pines and put my grip down. Shut off by those sweet-smelling trees, their tops moving just a little in the breeze, I felt I was a hundred miles from that red clay road. If it hadn't been for those darned pigs squealing, there wouldn't have been any sound at all except those pine limbs moving above me.

Pretty soon Geraldine came out the back door carrying two Royal Crown Colas. When I wrapped my hand around that big cold drink I wished that I had been thoughtful enough to bring her a present of some kind. But I don't know what it would have been, and I hadn't really been sure that I was going to see her at all.

She sat down on the needles, spreading that white skirt around her in a circle. She took a sip from her drink and smacked her lips. I raised my bottle up and felt the Cola cool and tickly down my throat.

"You got yourself a nice tan down in Jackson," she said. "I'll bet you went swimming every day."

"I didn't swim at all. I worked on a construction job, helping my daddy build a brick house."

"Goodness, you're a regular working man already."

"I guess not."

She giggled a little bit. "Did you practice your speech any?"

"I sure did. About every chance I had. Tomorrow's the big day."

"I'd like to be there to see you get that gold medal."

"I wish you could be."

She looked into my eyes, but it wasn't like the time back on Monday when we had been trying to outstare each other at first. Now I didn't feel any embarrassment looking at her at all.

All at once she smiled. "I quit chewing toothpicks."

"You look better without them." Then after a second or two I said, "But you look so good anyhow that the toothpicks didn't really hurt. Did you ever go back to school?"

"Uh huh. I went back on Wednesday and school was out on Friday. I'm through with the eighth grade now."

I started to say that I was through with the ninth, but she knew that. Besides, I wasn't thinking much about school. I looked at those pretty white arms and that fine chest rising beneath those red flowers printed on that white blouse. I tried and tried, but I couldn't remember for the life of me what that fine titty had really looked like last Monday morning. And the rest of it, those long white legs and that black hair-patch, I just couldn't picture at all. Even though I could see something like a hair-patch in my mind all right, it wasn't really Geraldine's but actually closer to a picture maybe, probably of one of those nudist things that J. D. Stuckey went around shoving under everybody's face. Now, with that white skirt spread in a circle and that red-flowered blouse, she was like some kind of peppermint stick rising out of a spread of white icing. And I felt strong, really strong, like I could chin one of those pines a hundred times or maybe run without stopping those seven miles or so on into Wesley.

I said, "Will you still give a penny for my thoughts?"

She actually blushed a little bit. "You crazy thing, you. You know something? You act different from what you did before."

"Not too different, I hope."

"Oh, no, it's all right. But you do seem different—like older maybe."

"Well, I am. Six days older."

"Oh, you silly."

"Look, I thought about you a lot this week."

"I thought about you too."

152

"Why?"

"Why what?"

"I mean—why should you think about me? I've been wondering don't you have a steady boyfriend. If you were at Wesley the boys would be fighting each other for the chance to sit and talk to you on Saturday nights."

A frown went across her forehead like a pencil mark on white paper. She said, "I don't have any boyfriends at all. At school I can talk to a few boys, but they don't ever get to come see me."

"Why?"

"I told you before. My papa won't let them come here. He thinks I'd let them screw me."

That one darned word. She'd drop it into the conversation as easy as a farmer mentioning the price of cotton. Just her saying it made me start turning hard. I looked straight at her. "Would you?"

"You have changed."

"Would you?"

"I don't know. It would depend on the boy."

Now I was hard as a railroad spike and really embarrassed—in a way. I put my hand in my pocket to try to get ahold of the situation. If only I could turn time back to that Monday morning, now that Floyd wasn't sitting in that red Ford blaring on the horn. We seemed just as far from everything else as we had then, maybe more so since the evening shadows were settling and the absolutely only sounds were a pig grunting and a chicken squawking now and then. But she was covered up now. Everything so mysterious was under that white circle of her skirt. It seemed dirty to think of trying to put my hand under that skirt.

She said, "Well?"

"Well what?"

"Oh, good gosh." Suddenly she stretched herself back on the pine needles. She kept her skirt down, but not all the way. I felt like biting her on the knees. But I didn't.

She said, "Did you ever play post office?"

"Yes. But I didn't like it too much."

"You didn't like it?"

"Well, I didn't especially care for any of the girls involved. One of them kept pushing her tongue out when we kissed. Gosh, it was like she was spitting. I mean really nasty."

"They call that French kissing."

"Then I think the American way is best. I certainly wouldn't use some girl's toothbrush, so why should I kiss her like that?"

She propped on one elbow and looked up at me. "Sometimes I don't know what in the world to think of you. I wish you wouldn't make a big problem out of everything."

"You asked me if I had played post office. I told you the truth."

"Would you like to play with me?"

"American way?"

"American way."

"Yes, I would."

"Well, I've got this big special delivery letter for you."

I moved over and sat down beside her. Her dark hair and eyes and those pink lips against that white skin made as pretty a picture as I ever saw. It was like one of these new Technicolored movies—everything prettier and brighter than colors really are. But I did wish I couldn't hear those pigs grunting.

She said, "Don't you want that special delivery letter?"

"I sure do."

"Well, get it right here."

I leaned over and pressed my lips against hers. They were soft and moist and warm. I don't remember how far back it was that I first wanted to kiss a girl, but it was plenty early. So I had kissed a lot of girls, but this was different. I had never been really off by myself with a girl like this—one who seemed to know what she was doing.

I didn't keep my lips against hers but a few seconds. She said, "That was the shortest special delivery ever. You still owe me ten cents postage. I don't think you really know how to play post office."

"I guess I don't."

I leaned over her again. This time when my lips came against hers she put her arms around my neck and squeezed real tight. I wasn't sure I could do everything, but at least I could hug her the way she hugged me. Our noses were breathing real fast. And I didn't wait for her to do it for me this time—I put my hand out to one of those fine titties and pressed it through that red-flowered cloth. She really breathed fast then.

I sort of settled down there like I was planning to keep kissing till Christmas. I didn't know what else to do. Of course, I had run part way around that track before—you know, the titty-squeezing and the hair-patch pressing that I had done before with her, back on Monday. But I didn't really know where to go from there, so I kept kissing and squeezing.

Finally, all on my own, I slipped my hand between the buttons on her blouse and my fingers felt that warm smooth titty. Then I undid the buttons, and my fingers went to one of those red tips, and I remembered something I heard Bob Durham say at the dorm one day. I rolled that little tip and squeezed it.

"Not so hard! You think you're pulling the head off a chicken?"

"I'm sorry."

"I didn't say stop, silly. Just not so hard."

It was so exciting that I couldn't help thinking how nice it would be getting a chance to do something like this every day. But I don't know, it sure wouldn't leave time for much else. And if a boy squeezed titties all the time he'd probably get to where he wouldn't care much for it at all.

That Geraldine was sure a sly one, though. I had been kissing and kissing—so much, in fact, that I was getting a little tired of it. It *was* hard to breathe with our noses jammed up against each other's like that. But right when I started feeling that the kissing was getting humdrum, I'll be darned if she didn't start rubbing the tip of her tongue on my lips. And pretty soon—I couldn't really help myself—I touched hers with mine and it didn't seem nasty at all. Not like using another person's toothbrush at all—once you got used to it.

Gosh, she was really squirming! I was lying alongside her and, hard like I was, I pressed against her hip and she was actually kind of wriggling on those brown needles.

She probably thought I was never going to get around to doing all the necessary things. Pretty soon she grabbed my hand and put it on her hip. My hand was just above her knee under the skirt, and I started running that hand along that smooth leg, cool as silk. I kept expecting to run into her bloomers, but I didn't. When I found she wasn't wearing any, I really started feeling confident.

My hand wandered in that dark brush, and my fingers slipped down as her legs came apart. She reached down and pulled that full white skirt up all the way to her chin. And there it was again. It hadn't really changed in the six days since I first saw it. It looked just the way it had looked, but now it had all the details in the flesh that my mind hadn't been able to fill in. Now I remembered where she'd told me to rub before. I rubbed. Her legs went wider. I rubbed some more. I was breathing so hard it was almost like I was in that fight with those bricklayers again. I racked my mind for all the information I'd picked up about this—stuff that J.D. and Bob and Allison and Warren Anderson always talked about, stuff that I had seen in those filthy pictures, and what I remembered from that glance I had at Floyd and Mrs. Wester.

I didn't take my trousers off, but just undid the buttons and let myself pop out. And I sure popped. I felt strong enough to whip Louis and Schmeling and Max Baer in one night, with Jimmy Braddock thrown in for good measure. I was against her white hip. I couldn't help but look down there and think how wonderful it felt for that part of me to be against that beautiful skin that way. I really do love beautiful skin. Right then I would have liked to be Solomon and David and have a ton of concubines like Geraldine and V. Mae to press against.

I knew I was a gone sinner, and even when I made a half-hearted try to think about John Gabriel and Howard Williams and the other evangelists' warnings I just couldn't seem to get bothered. But it's no wonder that they devote such special attention to this kind of thing, because I can see where a person could sure make it a habit—if he wasn't careful.

I just wasn't careful at all. That part of me was pressing between her legs and I was bouncing up and down like I was riding a jogging horse. I could feel the very tip of me pushing at her, singing its way through that black hair and feeling sharper all the time, keen as a razor being whetted on a barber's strop. I wasn't sure yet what I was doing. I just wanted to push and push and feel and feel. But I was as awkward as old Primo Carnera pushing his lumbering left arm out at Max Baer. I knew there was a target somewhere down there, but I wasn't sure if I was hitting it or not. But it felt good.

"Oh, gosh," she said. "Gosh."

I bounced some more and dug in like a football tackle leading the way through the line. I'll bet if I'd been playing ball then I could have bumped aside big guys like Willie Jefferson with no effort at all.

I gave one tremendous jab. The pain shot through me. I sort of hissed and stopped short.

She said, "What's wrong?"

"I—I don't know. Something hurt."

Pulling back, I saw the tip of one of those stiff pine needles stuck in me. I had gone down between her legs and hit the ground.

She said, "Well, I swear. You're not doing it right yet."

I felt her fingers around me, holding onto me down there.

She said, "Go ahead now."

I pushed again, and this time I was into something so hot and smooth-soft that I stopped again. I knew that this was it. And my face was beside hers and I smelled the sweet skin of her neck and I felt the solid softness of her chest against mine and I didn't move so fast anymore because now I could feel the great heat circling me and going through me like standing before a glowing red side of a stove on a cold morning. When I moved again, her mouth was up against my ear and her tongue was touching my ear and if I'd been the red line in a thermometer I would have shot up and up, beyond the tops of those pine trees.

Yet, all the time I was watching myself. I was another part of me, backed away, watching calm but interested in what I was doing. I pulled my head over hers and looked at her face. She opened her eyes and smiled. I kissed her and her mouth was open against mine and then I was moving and she was moving and there was nothing in the world but us and the stove got hotter and the thermometer went higher and we moved faster and faster and her arms were almost choking me and I wanted to stop but I couldn't. The pressure built like a balloon getting bigger and bigger to the bursting point and the end is suddenly turned loose and the thing shoots up and around and over in one great blast till everything is gone.

Warm and sticky, still and close, I lay there. It was drifting along, floating on your back in creek water, tired from swimming but still enjoying the way the water pushes your body up.

In a minute or so I started to move again.

She said, "No. Get up."

I still wanted to move. She said, "Get up. You're going to get your pants all dirty."

I hadn't thought about that. I rolled away from her and put my handkerchief around me and tucked myself in. She dropped her dress and started to get up.

I said, "Don't get up yet."

"We have to. I don't know how soon Mama and Papa will be back."

"If they went to church they sure won't be back just yet."

"They didn't go to church. They might be back any minute."

That was different. I felt funny then, kind of like the empty balloon lying on the ground with all the air gone. I said, "You should have told me. If your papa found me I'd be in real trouble."

"Well, you'd better hurry now."

"I don't want to run off just yet."

"You'd better."

"You mean go right now?"

"I'm sorry, but you have to."

I looked at her. Her face seemed softer, more relaxed than it had been, but there was something harder about it too. She reminded me a lot of her mama just then. But she was still very pretty.

I said, "Tomorrow night I'll be leaving Wesley and I won't be back for the rest of the summer. I won't see you for a long time."

"I know. Are you sorry?"

"Of course I'm sorry I won't see you."

"Are you sorry you screwed me?"

"I wish you'd find some other word for that."

"I don't know another word but one. And that sounds worse to me."

She was right about that. I nodded my head. It does seem bad, though, that something which feels as good as that did has to be talked of in such nasty language.

She said, "Well, are you sorry?"

"Don't keep asking me that. If you liked it I'm not sorry."

"It was wonderful."

"I think so too."

She put her arm round my waist and hugged me again. Then she said, "You hadn't really ever done it before, had you?"

"Not really. Not but once. And I guess I didn't really do it then."

"I have. I've done it quite a few times."

"I thought so. Who with?"

"My cousin. He spent three weeks with us last summer."

Good gosh! A fine cousin! I didn't say anything.

She said, "But I liked you the best."

That was something anyway. I said, "Thanks."

I heard the loud motor of a car coming from the direction of Wesley. I jumped at first, afraid I might be missing a ride, but if it was coming from Wesley it wouldn't do me any good.

But she grabbed my arm. "Run! Run behind the barn and cut across through the woods."

"Is that your papa?"

"It might be. Hurry. He's feeling pretty upset right now."

"What do you mean—feeling upset?"

"He had to go meet the sheriff at Floyd's house. That's where he's been—and Mama too."

"At Floyd's house?"

She looked at me and didn't blink an eye. "They found Floyd dead in his car last night. Somebody shot him."

When the blood stopped freezing in my brain, I said, "Was it your papa? Did he kill Floyd?"

"I don't know. I don't know if Papa did it or not."

The sound of the motor was louder. I looked down and saw a stain at the fly of my trousers, where I'd had them unbuttoned. I kissed her real fast and picked up the grip and ran behind the barn. Lucky, it was getting almost dark, and when that car rumbled up the little road to Geraldine's house I was sure that nobody could see me. But I tried to save time by cutting across the pig lot. I was glad I didn't have on Daddy's fine shoes then. That black piggy ooze came squashing up around my tennis shoes and that filthy smell was enough to turn a man's stomach. I was ankle deep in that filth before I climbed the rail fence and made it to the woods.

ELEVEN

It's STRANGE how a person knows some things. Even though Floyd had just nodded and beeped his horn at the little old lady on the porch, I knew, the morning we drove past, that it was his house. It was only about a mile and a half out of Wesley. Now I could see Floyd's red car pulled up at the side of the yard along with six or seven others. I shivered a little bit, knowing that Floyd would never drive that red Ford again.

I couldn't reason out why I was stopping there now, but I think I knew I was going to from the first minute Geraldine told me Floyd was dead. That's very strange too. Imagine her knowing a thing like that and not saying a word to me about it until—until that other was all over—well, all right, until I'd screwed her. That's the way she'd put it, and I might as well be honest myself. I had sure enough screwed a girl, no doubt about that. And for the past two and a half hours, while I stomped up and down those dark clay hills, the knowledge of my sin had been riding me like an ape on a bare-backed mule. About four or five cars passed me going back toward McCool, but not a one came by going the other way. With that little brown grip scraping the side of my leg, I kept repeating the 23rd Psalm, especially "Yea, though I walk through the valley of the shadow of death, I will fear no evil: for thou art with me." It wasn't that I was actually scared of anything there in the night, but I was feeling bad about Floyd and myself, what I'd done. I suppose I was a pretty bad bet then for getting God to walk with me through that valley, but somehow I was hoping that somebody had walked with Floyd.

Right after I plunged into the woods from Geraldine's place I found a little creek. Because of the dry weather it wasn't too full, but the water was running fairly clear. I took my trousers and underwear shorts off and washed my lower parts, rubbing mud on and packing it around and then rinsing the mud off. I stared at myself down there, sort of hard-pressed to understand that I had really done it. Yet I didn't really look any different. Then I stepped with my tennis shoes into that good clean creek mud and tried to wash some of that pig filth from my feet and shoes. I did manage to get most of it off and I felt a little better when I left the creek, but I could see the dark stain about an inch above the soles. It had soaked in so much that I knew it would never go away.

Well, no matter how dirty I was on the inside, at least I was a little cleaner on the outside when I left the road and walked toward Floyd's house. As I got closer I could hear people singing "The Old Rugged Cross." That startled me so much that I stopped short for a minute, not sure whether to go on up to the house or not. I had expected that several people might be there, but I just didn't figure on hymn-singing coming through the night from Floyd's home.

The porch light was burning, the bugs circling and buzzing, smacking themselves against that naked bulb. I knocked on the door.

The singers' voices were strong and clear, almost all women.

> To the old rugged cross I will ever be true,
> Its shame and reproach gladly bear,
> Till He calls me some day to my home far away,
> Where His glory forever I'll share.

The door opened. I was so surprised I almost said "Mother Joan" before I saw it wasn't her at all but a little lady dressed in black with the same kind of white hair and glasses. But there was one big difference I noticed right away. Where Mother Joan's eyes always seemed sad and hurt—like she was about to cry—this little lady had eyes that sparkled like a frosty field on a sunshiny morning.

She said, "Well, howdy, son."

"Good evening, ma'am. I'm Mark Torrance—from the academy."

"Oh, yes, another one of Floyd's friends. We had a right smart of the school boys over this afternoon—after they brought Floyd back from the undertaker in Kosciusko."

"Yes ma'am, I was Floyd's friend. Are you his mama?"

"Oh, no, goodness! I'm his grandma. You come in, son."

I slid my grip off to the side of the door and followed her into a long hall. From a little side parlor the singers were heading into the last verse of "The Old Rugged Cross." Looking in there, I saw eight or nine ladies sitting in a circle of straight-backed chairs while Reverend Estes from the Baptist church in Wesley led their singing. Mr. Estes was a heavyset man with a round happy face and gray-black hair. I wondered why Mr. Ingram wasn't there. I don't know whether Floyd belonged to any church or not; I had certainly never seen him in one; but, after all, he had played a lot of football for Wesley and it did seem that Reverend Ingram should have been there. Not that Reverend Estes wasn't just as good, I suppose—and a fine singer too.

Floyd's grandma said, "They're singing hymns for our boy."

"Yes ma'am."

As we stood there, listening to the last verse and the chorus, I wasn't sure whether I was expected to join in or not. But the grandma did. She had a high kind of tinny voice, reminding me again of the earnest way Mother Joan would sing at the prayer band. When they got to the chorus where it goes "So I'll cling to the old rugged cross," Mr. Estes came in strong and deep on the bass part, the words "That old cross!" rumbling under the sounds of the ladies.

When they finished singing, the ladies in the circle all looked at me. Floyd's grandma said, "It's another one of Floyd's friends from the school."

Mr. Estes shook my hand. "My, but it's late for you to be away from your dormitory, isn't it, boy?"

"No sir, not really. I'm just getting in from Jackson."

He looked like he was going to say something else, but he didn't. He turned to the ladies, said "Page eighty-three" and they flipped the pages in the hymn books and started on "Rock of Ages."

I was glad Floyd's grandma didn't stay to sing that one too. She took my arm and walked me down the hall like an usher taking me to a movie seat. The house was clean and nice, a pretty expensive and well-kept place smelling of furniture polish and wax, even though the carpet in the hall was worn a good bit.

We stopped at the door to a big kitchen. I didn't want to stick my head in there and act nosy, but Floyd's grandma sort of planted me there in the doorway. Over at the stove a big Negro woman was cooking and sweating. The smell of sausage grease hung cloudy in the room. Six men sat at the table, smoking and talking, drinking cups of coffee. I recognized two of them—Zack Banning, who had a drugstore and soda fountain in Wesley, and A. C. Fair, who ran a general store that sold everything from horse collars to BVD's.

Zack looked at me. "Why, it's a Torrance boy." He knew me because whenever I had a spare nickel I always bought chocolate ice cream cones at his fountain, but I don't think he knew my first name at all. Carl and I looked a lot alike.

Zack said, "What are you doing out from school this time of night, Torrance boy?"

"I'm just getting in from Jackson, Mister Banning. I had to walk over from McCool."

"Done took yourself a trip, have you?"

"Yes sir."

The other men nodded and puffed their pipes and cigarettes.

As if she knew there was nothing else to be said, Floyd's grandma put her hand on my arm. I turned with her and we walked back up the hall to a room across from the singers. They were still going strong. Floyd's grandma pulled a green curtain back at the door to the other room. Right away I saw the gray metal casket across the room. All the window drapes were pulled shut, and the casket sat on a long table with five big flower wreaths planted around it. That sickly sweet flower smell reminded me of the time two years before when my little cousin lay in that casket at the Tom E. Taylor funeral home in Jackson.

The room was very dark except for two lamps, one of them fixed so that the light hit Floyd's face where that half of the casket lid was turned back. About six feet off to the end of the casket, the end that was open, a woman in a black dress sat, rocking slow and steady, like the pendulum on a great clock.

The grandma pointed to the casket. "He's over there."

"Yes ma'am."

"I know you want to see him. You go right ahead."

The way she said it, it was just like I was supposed to have a private conversation with Floyd and she didn't intend to bother me. I suppose, in a way, I did want to have a talk with Floyd—at least in my mind.

I looked at the woman rocking so slowly—gently, softly, like she had a baby in her arms that I couldn't see. Her face was set hard, her eyes staring straight ahead at the casket but she didn't really seem to be seeing anything.

The grandma said, "That's Floyd's mama."

I about half nodded toward the lady in the chair, but she didn't make any sign that she even saw us. Glazed as a frozen window pane, those eyes probably wouldn't have noticed if fifteen or twenty people had walked in front of her. She seemed to be seeing something that was a long ways off from anything in that room.

I looked into the casket. During the months that I'd been seeing Floyd around town and school I don't believe I'd ever seen him dressed in anything except khaki trousers and white shirts and his old brown felt hat. During cold weather he wore a leather jacket, and I suppose he must have had heavier trousers on then too—probably tan corduroys. But now he lay there in a blue serge suit with a red tie around his neck. His left arm was down along his side but the right crossed his chest, his palm flat over his heart like he was about to pledge allegiance to the flag. His face was so prettified that it didn't seem like Floyd at all when I first looked. His jaw had always seemed fat and round, especially if he was packing a wad of tobacco, but now he looked lean-faced, the skin light and waxy-colored except right on his cheekbones, which were all reddened up like the cheeks of an expensive Christmas doll.

"He looks peaceful, don't he?" the grandma said.

"Yes ma'am."

There was the faintest trace of a smile the way his pinked-up lips were formed, and with his eyes closed he seemed to be thinking, like he was maybe about to spring loose with one of his WPA jokes.

The grandma said, "Freed from all earthly sorrow and affliction."

"Yes ma'am."

But, remembering old Floyd, I knew he hadn't really thought of life as any affliction—if he ever thought about anything at all besides selling those insurance policies and delivering the U. S. mail. I looked at that clean-parted blond hair, the darkened eyebrows, the girl-pink lips, and that darned tie knotted under his Adam's apple. It just didn't seem like that flush-faced sweaty-skinned man I remembered from our ride a few days before. And then the idea started to grow on me that this really wasn't Floyd anymore. "Ashes to ashes—dust to dust," the Bible said. Floyd was going back to the dead clay that God made Adam from. But this clay that was left now, this body that would later crumble to dust—it just wasn't Floyd at all. That prettified blue-serge solemn thing—I couldn't picture it doing all the things

Floyd had done or even some of the things that I had seen him do.

I didn't really know I was crying. I certainly hadn't made a sound. But when my hand went up to rub away a tear, that little old grandma squeezed my arm.

"I'll leave you here by yourself," she said. "I'll leave you with your own thoughts."

Well, there were sure a lot of those thoughts that I couldn't seem to get straight at all, and I wasn't too sure that this was the time to be trying to sort them all out. But she backed away from the casket, then moved silent as a shadow out of the room. I glanced at the mother. For all she seemed to know or care, I could have been a handle on the casket.

So Floyd wasn't really in that casket at all. What was left of the body was there—the body that could have got him a scholarship at Ole Miss or L.S.U. even. But soon there wouldn't be any more left of Floyd than was left now of that great L.S.U. supporter, Huey P. Long, sleeping in that Baton Rouge tomb that was spotlighted so bright in the darkness you could see the glow from miles around. Floyd's spirit had put away the flesh. I could understand that all right, but I just couldn't seem to really grab hold of the notion that the spirit just wasn't going to be around anymore. A few weeks ago I had made a report in English class on *King Lear,* and I had almost cried when I read some of those lines at the last when the old king is standing there with his dead daughter in his arms saying, "No, no, no life! Why should a dog, a horse, a rat, have life and thou no breath at all? Thou'lt come no more, never, never, never, never, never!" And now old Floyd would come no more. I didn't want to be silly or anything. I knew this. And yet, in a way, I didn't really know it.

Floyd had left the body behind. Where was the spirit now? According to Mrs. Mahan, there were only the two places. Floyd had either made it to Heaven or else he was roasting in Hell—there wasn't any in-between. And Floyd was a sinner, probably committing adultery right up to the very last. I didn't know who shot him or why, but he probably had women besides Mrs. Wester buying those insurance policies from him. But that was just the way Floyd lived. You might say that he couldn't anymore help being what he was than Mr. Lance Godbold could help being the fine evangelist that he was. I sure wished I could have talked to Lance Godbold right then. Mr. Estes was in that other room, booming away on those songs, but he never struck me as digging very deep into spiritual problems. I mean, if a person felt like singing all the time, then he wouldn't ever develop any problems.

But I just refused to picture Floyd in Hell—no more than I could have pictured my daddy in Hell if he'd gotten killed fighting those bricklayers. I knew I was probably sinning by not accepting the notion of Floyd being in hellfire, but I just couldn't do it.

I started to pray, but it was hard to know what to say. I said, "Dear God, Floyd's grandma said that he was free now of all earthly sorrow and affliction. I really don't know about that, but I wish You could find it in your heart to do what You can for Floyd. Lord, I realize I don't have much right to be asking favors at this time, considering what I did with Geraldine a few hours ago. But I hope You understand. Thank You, dear God. Amen."

That sure had me all jammed up again. I had started to say "Forgive me," but when I started thinking about Geraldine again I couldn't really say whether I was sorry or not now. It would be very hypocritical to ask forgiveness for something you didn't really regret. I had felt sorry enough about Geraldine right at first when she told me to hurry and leave, and I had certainly felt plenty sinful while I was padding up and down those dark clay hills, but now it was very hard to get straight. I guess the further away a boy gets from screwing a woman like that, the better it seems.

I looked at that poor mother, rocking and staring. I nodded to her again, but she didn't see me so I backed on out of the room.

The little grandma was waiting in the hall, standing by the door, singing "Shall We Gather at the River?", the song Mr. Estes was leading in the little parlor.

She stopped singing and came up to me in the hall. "Won't you stay and have some late supper?"

"Ma'am?"

"We're going to have a little bite to eat."

"Thank you, ma'am. I wouldn't really care for any food."

We stopped by the front door. She said, "You're a sweet boy to come by and see Floyd."

"I just had to see him. I liked Floyd an awful lot."

"I hope you'll come to the funeral. Tomorrow afternoon at three o'clock—right out here in the family plot."

"I'd sure like to come to the funeral. But I have to take part in a program at the school tomorrow afternoon."

She put her flaky white hand on my arm. "You're a sweet boy. God bless you."

"Goodbye, ma'am. God bless your home."

I eased out the door and picked up the grip. I walked down the porch steps and headed toward the road. Back in the parlor the singers finished their song. Then I heard the Negro cook's voice loud and clear, "Flapjacks and sausage is ready." Several of the ladies in that front parlor spoke at the same time, the words mingling so that I couldn't understand all they were saying, but it sounded like they were ready to eat.

Flapjacks and sausage! I guess Mr. Estes decided to hold them off the food a little while longer, because they started singing "Nearer My God to Thee."

TWELVE

Up on the stage Reverend Ingram's face played games, his eyes growing wider behind the outlines of his black glasses and black eyebrows. His brown skin shone from all the talking, his teeth bright now and then in a smile. A visiting school superintendent from Attala County had just given the diplomas to the fourteen members of the graduating class.

"And now," said Mr. Ingram, "it seems to me there was some other announcement to be made before the program ends. But I seem to have forgotten what it is."

As the audience giggled, he paused and smiled, his eyes seeming to search me out as he looked through that crowd of three hundred people crammed into the auditorium. Then he said, "Ah, yes, it seems to me that I have an announcement that will be of vital interest to three young gentlemen."

He was sure enjoying himself. I smiled too, appreciating his humor, just relaxing and letting the good feeling roll all through me. Sitting back on the last row of the center section, I could see several people up forward, especially in the side sections, twisting around slightly to sort of glance back my way. They were all smiling.

Everybody seemed to be smiling at me after the contest. It had been a strangely good day—especially to follow such a god-awful night as I had just gone through. First of all, it had been good to ease into the room around midnight and wake up Carl and John and talk to them. But I hadn't really told them much about all that had happened to me. There are some things that you can't tell—not even to a brother. That business between Mama and Daddy I would certainly never tell Carl; it couldn't do anything but hurt him. I did mention the fight at the Shady Rest bootleg joint, but the strangest thing of all was that I didn't tell Carl and John about my adventure with Geraldine and Floyd. Sometime, later, I would probably tell Carl, but right then I felt like a wiser man for deciding not to speak of it right away.

Naturally, everybody at school knew Floyd was dead, but there certainly didn't seem to be too much excitement about it. Some of the older boys, Bob Durham and Walt Hunter especially, had been pretty hard-faced about it, but that was about all. Even Bob said that Floyd was involved with so many women that the law wouldn't have half a chance to find out who shot him.

Still, while I was sitting on that stage at three in the afternoon, waiting with Warren and Allison to deliver those declamations, I kept thinking that only a mile and a half away a former Wesley football star was about to be lowered into the ground—the end of a life. Yet here was a big crowd waiting for three kids to stand up and make some talks that—when you consider life and death—didn't really amount to much at all. Of course, my speech on capital punishment was certainly interesting and dramatic and very timely, but Allison had one called "The Southern Heritage" and poor Warren's was even worse—something called "League of Nations, World Hope for Security," a topic that was just about null and void now that the League had let Italy run over Ethiopia.

The deep booming hum of Mr. Ingram's voice rolled round the auditorium. No matter how monotonous his voice got sometimes, it sure had carrying power. He said, "It is my pleasant duty to declare a winner of the declamation contest. And—"

My breath started coming faster, and I smiled again, waiting.

Next to me Mama patted my knee and smiled. On the other side of her, Daddy leaned toward Carl and said something, but I couldn't hear what it was.

Mr. Ingram said, "And I hereby declare that the winner of this contest is—" he paused for a long time, staring out over the audience like John Barrymore in some kind of pose—"the winner of that contest is—right here in this room."

The audience really laughed at that. Mr. Ingram smiled some more, very pleased no doubt with the way he was building the suspense in the room.

Mama and Daddy had come driving in from Jackson at practically the last minute—I mean, really out of the blue just before the contest started. In fact, I was already sitting on stage with Warren and Allison when I saw them come through the doors at the rear of the auditorium with Carl and John. And, really, I had just been sitting there hoping they would. My folks do very unpredictable things, and this was just like them. It really charged me up. You see, Warren Anderson's folks had come down from Memphis and it made me wish for my own folks to be there. The Andersons were distinguished-looking people, supposed to have a little money. Warren had been to a couple of other schools, fancy ones like Gulf Military, and he said his folks would send him anyplace he wanted to go. Mr. Anderson was a tall thin man, wearing a fine brown Palm Beach suit. His wife had gray hair, but she still looked young and sure of herself. Warren was dressed in some very sharp blue trousers with white coat and white shoes. Even Allison had on a pretty nice suit. I looked down at my feet dressed in those creamy-tan vented shoes that Daddy had given me. I felt better then, even though I wasn't wearing a coat—just a white shirt and bow tie and some new light-gray trousers.

Before Mama and Daddy came into the auditorium I had been sitting on that stage feeling so strangely happy and sad at the same time. I felt like something was slipping away from me. Maybe it was just the ending of the school year, but it seemed like more than that. In some ways I didn't feel like myself anymore. There I was with all those thoughts bottled up in me—thoughts about Floyd in his casket, my body on Geraldine, Lance Godbold and his sick baby, all those bricklayers white and black, and my own folks. I looked at those faces in the audience, knowing that all those heads had their own private thoughts that never could be told to another. It kind of scared me in a way, and yet it really shouldn't have. It was just something that I had never really considered seriously before—so many people, and all of them so different.

Back in the left wing of the stage, before the contest started, I had been studying the initials and dates carved and written into the walls. Some of the dates went back to 1880—about the time my own daddy was born. I wondered how far into the years those dates would run before the old building was torn down. While I was thinking about that, Warren Anderson, who was pretty nervous, started singing very softly:

> *Columbus sailed past San Salvador*
> *In search of golden booty.*
> *And on the shore he spied a whore,*
> *My God, she was a beauty.*

Allison McGee began to laugh. Luckily, Miss Hunter stuck her head back about that time and said we should go out to the stage and sit down. If she hadn't, no telling how long Warren would have kept singing, trying to calm his nerves.

Mr. Ingram cleared his throat. "That boy and two others a few short hours ago treated an audience to such magnificent displays of oratory as have seldom been witnessed in this auditorium."

The audience laughed again. Then somebody decided it might be polite to applaud. Everybody joined in.

I don't know that an honest man could really call those speeches "magnificent displays" at all. I had almost fallen out of my chair when I saw Mama and Daddy coming in back there. But I just looked across those rows of people very coolly and smiled slightly. Daddy gave a big grin and raised his arms with their half-rolled sleeves over his head and clenched his hands together like a fighter being introduced in the ring. Mama nudged him and he took his straw hat off and sat down.

Allison McGee had led off the program. I was very relieved as his eight minutes went by. He had managed to work on the speech enough that he didn't forget anything, but he was awful mechanical the way he talked. It was so obvious that he was just rattling something off from memory. When he finished and turned to walk back to his seat he winked at me as if to say he was plenty glad it was all over.

Then Warren Anderson got up. Even though he wasn't quite sixteen he already had to shave almost every day. He was a nice-looking guy with a fine deep voice, but he had never been really serious about the contest and I knew he was going to have trouble. He hadn't gone two minutes before he started stumbling over some words and had to go back and repeat them. A little later he made a move to his left, started to raise his hand the way he'd been coached to do, and then seemed to change his mind. He had an expression like a diver in mid-air who looks down and sees no water in the lake. All in all, Warren messed up quite a few things. I looked at his fine-looking folks out in the audience, and I was sure embarrassed for them. A boy with a good voice like that—too lazy to take the time and trouble to practice his speech!

You might say that the contest really ended when Warren sat down. I had been a little nervous myself, but after that demonstration by Warren and Allison I knew that I could do better even if I had to walk around on my hands while I was talking. The old confidence just zoomed through me. I gave that speech the best I ever said it in my life, squeezing those dramatic sections so hard that I'll bet the folks out front could see those quivering trembling bodies dangling from the end of ropes. When I sat down I got twice the applause that either Allison or Warren got. Back at the rear of the auditorium I could see Mama and Daddy smiling and clapping their hands.

174

Mr. Ingram said, "And the winner of that contest is . . ."

We all held our breath again. I smiled and waited. Mr. Ingram fumbled around his coat pocket. Then he said, "My, I seem to have lost the slip with the winner's name."

That was really funny to me! After all, if a man who had been one of the two judges didn't know who the winner was, then who did? The audience didn't laugh too much at that joke, so Mr. Ingram must have decided that he had stretched the thing far enough. I was getting a little impatient myself.

He extended his right arm, pointing his finger at the audience, but the arm kept moving, never staying pointed at one spot but just a few seconds.

"I hereby declare the winner of the declamation contest to be . . ."

The arm moved and the finger came my way. I was smiling, my legs tensing and my feet planted to stand up when the applause started.

The finger went past me and pointed toward the left down front.

"The winner is Warren Anderson."

THIRTEEN

WHEN WE passed Geraldine's house I was sunk so low in the back seat that I almost didn't notice. As it was, I just perked my head up a little and thought about the way she'd said she would like to be there to see me win that medal. Then I just dropped my head down again. I had hardly said a word since we got into the old Plymouth in front of the auditorium and left Wesley. Of course, I had managed, when the final prayer was said, to go up to Warren Anderson and congratulate him on winning the contest. I told him he deserved to win, and I guess he must have if Mr. Ingram and Miss McKinley thought he was the best. But I was in an awful state of confusion. During the few minutes before we got away from Wesley I avoided looking at people. My ears and face were burning, and I could imagine what they were all thinking, getting a big laugh at how fooled I was when Mr. Ingram announced the winner.

Carl seemed to be dozing over in his corner of the back seat. He hadn't said anything at all about the contest. I knew how disappointed Mama and Daddy were, but they hadn't said anything either. Mama just kept her hands on the wheel and her eyes on that curving dirt road from Wesley to State 12.

But as soon as we pulled out into that dark gravel of State 12, almost like it was some kind of signal, Daddy put his left arm on the seat and turned back to look at me. "All right, Mark," he said. "You're away from that goddam place now. You can stop crying."

"I'm not crying!"

Mama said, "Leave him alone. He's not crying."

"The hell he's not," Daddy said. "If you want to cry, boy, there's a lot more in this world to cry over than not winning a little gold medal. By God, there's a lot of medals in this world that I never won!"

Mama said, "God knows that's the truth."

I said, "I know it doesn't really amount to much. But I was so sure. Then I was surprised and embarrassed. Everybody thought *I* was going to win."

"*You* sure thought that," Daddy said. "You didn't see how it was possible for you to lose. Well, boy, I've been losing all my life." He looked back at Mama. "Now say 'God knows that's the truth' to that."

Mama said, "Leave Mark alone. He's in no humor to listen to all this talk."

"All what talk? I'm just telling him he has to learn how to lose. Don't you think a boy ought to know what it is to lose like a man by the time he's thirteen years old?"

I said, "I know how to lose, Daddy. But I can't understand *why* I lost. You know yourself that you and Mama and Carl and John—all of you thought that I won. You told me so right after the contest was over."

Mama said, "Yes, you were a lot better than the other two."

I said, "All right then, you see? I'll bet fifty people told me right after the contest that I was a cinch, that there—"

Daddy said, "There ain't no cinch in this goddam world."

Mama said, "That's just about enough of that kind of talk, Carl."

I said, "I just can't understand what the basis was for Mr. Ingram and Miss McKinley to make the decision. I just don't understand it."

Carl wasn't really asleep. From the dark corner he raised his head and looked over my way. He said, "Hell, Legs, they don't want to tell you, but I will."

Mama said, "Carl Junior, be careful what you say."

Carl said, "It won't hurt him to know a few things besides what they write in books. Look, Legs, Miss McKinley would vote for anybody as winner that Mr. Ingram told her to vote for—mainly because she wants to keep her job next year. And old Ingram himself was the other judge. So that's it."

I thought it sounded smart-alecky for Carl to say "old Ingram" like that, but Mama and Daddy didn't correct him, so I didn't either. I said, "All right, so Mr. Ingram was the real judge. So what? He's a good judge of speakers."

Carl said, "Yeah. And that's not all."

"What do you mean?"

"Did you notice where the Andersons sat at supper tonight?"

"Yes."

"And did you notice the snotty attitude Mrs. Mahan put on when we sat the folks down at her table?"

"She's a fine lady! She's never snotty!"

"Okay, Legs, that's all I'm saying. You just think about it."

It was like finding a couple of pieces of the jigsaw puzzle that had been lying there on the rug all the time. I remembered that Mr. Ingram and his wife had hardly said a word to Mama and Daddy, but Carl was right—the Andersons had sat at that head table with the Ingrams, and Mrs. Ingram and her daughter Betty Ruth had been smiling and chattering and preening themselves like a couple of strutting peacocks or whatever they call the female birds. And the more I thought about it, the more I decided that Carl might be right about Mrs. Mahan too. Not that she had really said anything out of the way to the folks. But she had seemed kind of unhappy, her face pretty stiff and unsmiling. I thought it was because Daddy wasn't really dressed as well as some of the other guests, like Mr. Anderson. Daddy's big neck had crunched that collar down to a pulp during that hot afternoon, his eye looked pretty black, and under those turned-up shirt sleeves his thick brown hands and wrists didn't look very delicate when he handled his food. And I remembered the look on Mrs. Mahan's face when Daddy paused while crunching his way through a piece of ham and said, "I had a brother made a fortune in Chicago in liquor and gambling, then lost it all trying to be an honest businessman—playing the stock market." And Mrs. Mahan had seemed to wince sometimes when Mama called her "hon" the way she always does other women, and when Mama told that she had taught piano back in Inverness when she was just sixteen years old, Mrs. Mahan had smiled as if to say she didn't really believe it but that she was too polite to call Mama a liar.

Suddenly I almost roared the words, "Why? Why would a man of God do a dishonest thing?!!"

"Money," Carl said from his dark corner. "Hellfire, Legs, money is the key to everything nowadays. That's right, huh, Daddy?"

"I don't say that exactly," Daddy said. "But I will say there's damned few doors money can't unlock."

I said, "Money? I still don't see why Mr. Ingram—"

"Wake up, Mark," Carl said. "Warren's bill was paid—that's for sure. Nobody had to send him home to get money from his folks."

I stared at Carl. "Who told you I did that?"

"Old Ingram called me in the office the very afternoon of the day you left. He wanted me to write a letter to Daddy dunning him for the money, but I didn't do it."

I said, "But I did. I went home in person and dunned him for all I was worth."

Mama said, "I've heard enough of this."

I said, "Daddy worked all last week as a scab to get money to pay the bill. It is paid now. Isn't it, Daddy?"

Daddy was looking ahead now, staring at that dark road in the moonlight. "We need money to live on. I couldn't give him all of it. We still owe the school twenty dollars."

"But, good gosh, you don't think—I mean, a man of God?"

Nobody answered me. I thought about that long rigmarole

that Mr. Ingram had gone through before he presented the medal. It had seemed funny to me when I thought I was going to win, but now I saw it all as a chance to humiliate me and the folks that Mr. Ingram just couldn't pass up.

"Well," I said, "I see it all now. I'm not too thick. It just takes a sledge hammer to break through my dumb head. All my practicing was for nothing. Because we owed the school money I never had a real chance to win."

Daddy said, "Not even if you could outtalk Clarence Darrow."

I slumped back in the seat. For a couple of minutes no one said anything. Then Daddy started talking about how he hoped the government would pay some kind of insurance dividend or bonus that summer to the veterans of the World War. I closed my eyes, thinking that a person sure never knows who he can trust in this world, knowing for sure that a person is always really pretty much by himself. Here I was in the car with the three people in the world who were closest to me, and yet they couldn't understand me and I couldn't understand them. We all loved each other, but we were so far apart.

Then, almost as if the last time I'd headed south over this road it had been a moonlight night instead of a hard bright dusty morning, I began to sense where we were, what we were approaching. Maybe he wouldn't even be there any more. Probably he had buried his baby and moved on. All at once I knew that I had to find out for certain if that child had died.

I sat up and leaned my head out the car window. "Slow down," I said. "Please slow down a little, Mama."

The car slowed very abruptly, as if Mama had taken her foot off the gas quickly, but then the speed picked up again as she gave some more gas. She said, "You scared the devil out of me, Mark. I'm not going fast in this old loose gravel. Not but forty. If I go any slower we'll be all night getting back to Jackson."

Daddy turned again and looked back at me. "What's wrong? You sick, boy?"

"No, I'm looking for something. Slow, Mama, please go slow. There it is—right up ahead—that little road to the left."

Mama slowed down. "What about that little road?"

"I want you to drive us about a hundred yards up that little road, Mama. I want to see a man I know—just for a minute."

Mama said, "My God, Mark—this time of night?"

Daddy said, "It's ten o'clock, boy. These country folks go to bed early."

I said, "Not this man. I'll bet he hardly ever sleeps."

Mama said, "This is no time of night for sensible people to be making visits, Mark."

"Please, Mama. This man may not even be home, may not even live here anymore."

"All right." Mama swung the car into the little road, stirring the chalky dust, and we drove up to the clearing on the right where Mr. Godbold lived. He was still there. His old Model-A was pulled up beside the shack. Through the screen door I could see some sort of dim light inside.

When Mama stopped the car I jumped out. "I'll be right back. Wait just a minute."

In the moonlight I could see Simon slinking out from under the steps.

Daddy said, "Watch out for that big black bastard."

Simon never even growled or barked. As I got closer he moved toward me, finally putting his wet nose against my fingers and his rough tongue on my palm. I walked up the four steps to the porch and knocked very softly at the side of the screen door.

I didn't try to peer through the screen door into that half-darkness, but I could see or feel that somebody was coming to the door. It was Mr. Godbold.

I said, "Hello, Mr. Godbold. I hope I didn't wake you up." His voice didn't sound surprised at all when he opened the door and stepped out to the porch. "Ah, yes, it's Mark come back for a visit. 'Seek ye the Lord while he may be found—' "

" 'Call ye upon him while he is near.' "

His strong right hand was grasping mine. "God love you, boy. You didn't waken me, but we must talk softly."

"Is Mrs. Godbold still sick?"

"Sleeping, lad, sleeping. She and the babe."

In the dark he leaned his face closer to mine as if he was reading the surprise I showed. "Don't be amazed at the power of the Lord, Mark. He made heaven and earth in six days. The babe lives. Lives and grows stronger. Come in."

I moved softly behind him as he entered the room. Two kerosene lamps were burning on the table next to the stove. He picked up one, and I waited until he led the way toward the bed. I noticed that the back window had been screened again, and there were several new things in the shack—bottles, brushes, diapers stacked up, and a little basket crib. Mr. Godbold had sure gone into the baby business.

He saw me looking at all the stuff. He said, "I'm a little embarrassed at all folks have done for us. My brother told some church people in Kosciusko and they brought it out to me. There's even talk of getting me a new car. But I won't hear of that."

"I don't see why not. It's no more than you and your family deserve—or need. You ought to take some church money and use it."

"I don't have a church, Mark. It would be God's money."

He held the lamp above the little crib. The baby was covered except for his head, and he was breathing easy, so soft you could hardly tell he was breathing at all—certainly not like all that wheezing and puffing that I had seen last time.

I said, "Thanks to the Lord for answering our prayer."

"Amen."

Then something seemed to crumble inside me. Catching his sleeve, I whispered for him to come outside to the porch again. Without a word he turned and followed me, closing the screen door very softly.

I said "I have to talk to you."

He looked down the way toward the black Plymouth sitting in the moonlight. "Are those your people in that car, lad?"

"Yes sir. My mama, daddy, and brother."

"You ought to ask them up to the house."

"Yes sir. In just a minute. First I have to tell you something."

"Sit down, Mark. Don't be pacing. You'll have poor Simon all excited."

We sat on the edge of the porch with our feet on the steps. He said, "You don't need to tell me what you've done. Tell it to the Lord."

"He already knows."

"Yes. Of that you may be sure."

"Mr. Godbold, when I saw you a week ago I was pure—well, reasonably pure. I had been tempted just before you picked me up, but I was still clean. Since that time, sir, I have known vanity, hatred, foolish pride, and lust for the flesh. To all of these I have fallen an easy prey—a simple weak sinner."

His face caught the glow from the moon when he tilted his head to look at me. "*All* of these, Mark?"

"All. Yes sir, every one. Tonight my pride was humbled, but because of that I've felt outrage, not repentance. A few days ago down in Jackson I struck a man with a pistol—hit him with blind murder in my heart. And I'm not sure I'm sorry. And just yesterday evening—yesterday evening, mind you—I had this carnal knowledge of a young girl. I took advantage of her."

His face showed just the slightest kind of tense expression and his dark forehead wrinkled up into the white. "How young a girl?"

"Fourteen."

The lines eased a little in his face. "Why, you're not that old yourself, son. Are you sorry?"

I gripped my hands together and looked out at the shining top of the black Plymouth, the old car sitting hard and dark, with the inside hidden, like the carload of souls it was carrying. I remembered the day I looked out the back window of the apartment and saw Mama go from the Plymouth to that other car. I remembered Daddy swinging that door open so he could step out and smash that bricklayer in the mouth.

"I don't know, Mr. Godbold. It's hard to say whether I'm

sorry or not. I'm pretty confused about a lot of things. Just a week ago I was pretty sure of myself and everything else."

"Do you love the girl, Mark?"

"I don't know. I love her in a way. I did love her while I was doing it." Geraldine would have said *screwing* right out to that fine evangelist, but I just couldn't shock him that way. "It gave me a feeling, some kind of power, that I never felt in me before."

"The power of creation, Mark. God's power."

"Yes, I guess that's it all right. But I guess I wasn't in love with the girl. Not really. Not the way David loved Bathsheba. Say, you know that was some sin he did when he had Uriah set up so he could be killed in battle? I mean, so he could get Bathsheba."

"Do you like to compare yourself to David?"

"Oh, no, I wouldn't do that."

"You might be like him. But remember that a big sin wasn't all he committed. He did big things for the Lord as well."

"That's right. I hadn't thought about that. People like David and Solomon kind of earned the right to take a few women, huh?"

His hand was on my back up around the neck. "Do you feel better for telling me all this, Mark?"

"Yes sir. But—don't you want to tell me something else?"

"I don't have the power to say go and sin no more, lad. I only say this. Talk to God. And may all your sins be sins of love. They're much the better kind."

I was about to say something else, but just then the horn on the Plymouth beeped very quickly and softly. I said, "They're getting a little impatient."

He stood up. "I don't preach hellfire and damnation, Mark. I preach love and understanding—for weakness as well as strength."

I said, "We ought to pray another prayer—a prayer of thanks-giving this time."

He said, "Would you like to do that, Mark?"

"Yes sir." I pointed toward the car. "I'd like to ask my folks to come up here and join us. Could I?"

"If you think they'd like."

I ran toward the car, hoping Mr. Godbold wouldn't follow me, because I wanted a chance to get a word in first. When I got to the car I glanced back and saw that he still stood at the top of the porch steps.

I leaned on the side of the car where Daddy was sitting. "Look," I said, "I want all of you to come up to the house for just a few minutes."

Mama said, "Who in the world lives there?"

"A man named Godbold. He's the well-known evangelist."

Daddy said, "That's the one who's nuts. Gives every dime he gets to charity."

I said, "Sssh, he might hear you."

Mama said, "How do you happen to know this preacher?"

"I'll tell you about that later. Right now we're about to say a prayer for his little baby that has been spared from death during the week since I first came down this road. We're going to thank God. Please come up there with us."

Mama said, "We can't spend no whole lot of time here, Mark. It's going to be late enough anyway when we get to Jackson."

"It won't take but a few minutes."

Mama and Daddy looked at each other. Then Mama turned to glance at Carl in the back seat. Carl said, "I don't mind. At school they keep us praying all the time."

Mama said, "I should certainly hope you'd pray anyway. It's the way I've trained you."

They got out of the car, and Mr. Godbold came down the porch steps, holding Simon away from us. Not that Simon would probably have done anything but sniff, but I was glad that he didn't get too close or Daddy might have called him a black bastard again.

While I was introducing Mr. Godbold, Mama kept nodding her head. She said, "Brother Godbold, I heard you preach a sermon in Inverness up in the Delta almost twenty years ago."

Mr. Godbold smiled and shook her hand. "Oh, yes, been there several times since. A fine place—Inverness. Nice little town."

"We're on our way to Jackson," Mama said. "This is a terrible time of night to drop in on folks."

Daddy nodded his head. "The boy wouldn't hear of us passing here without stopping."

Mr. Godbold smiled again. "He knows he's always welcome. And now he wants us all to pray together. Come inside and I'll show you why we're thanking God."

Then, while I held the door open, the three of them went in behind Mr. Godbold and passed around to the other side of the mattress where his wife was lying, that woman whose eyes I had never seen open, to the little white crib. The three of them stared at that little baby. Even Carl seemed surprised and concerned as he saw the smallness of that child. They talked so softly I couldn't tell what they were saying, but I could see Mama shaking her head over and over. She must have mentioned to Mr. Godbold that she wanted to touch the baby, because she put her hand out and a soft expression came over her face. Daddy had taken off his tie when he got in the car back in Wesley, and with his brown face and black hair and strong neck he looked much younger than usual in that lamplight.

Finally, without another word, Mr. Godbold turned and they all came back toward the door, except that this time Daddy waited till the last, still staring at that little baby. He stayed there so long that the rest of us were already out on the porch, and I had to go back to the door and wave for him to come on.

On the porch Mr. Godbold said softly, "Let's step out and pray beneath God's bright night sky."

We walked about halfway back to the car, then stopped and stood in a little circle. The dog Simon ambled his big black carcass along with us.

Mr. Godbold said, "Let's remain standing and bow our heads. I'll ask Mark to start the prayers. Then whoever likes can pray next. I'll wait for the rest of you and then I'll finish the prayer."

That piece of ground seemed like the quietest place on earth. Before I bowed my head and closed my eyes I thought how strange it seemed for all of us to be standing there in that particular place with our bodies throwing long shadows from the moonlight and that big black dog circling and sniffing us very softly now and then.

I kept my eyes closed for about thirty seconds. Then I said aloud, "Dear God, thank You for letting Mr. Godbold's baby live. May he grow strong and be a joy to his parents. Always remind our hearts, dear God, of the great things You can do." Then, since I had been thinking about Geraldine, "Lord, teach our hearts how to avoid sin. May we do as well as we can, Lord, and when we can't we ask You to please help and forgive us. Thank You again for the good health of this little baby. Amen."

I waited, hoping that Mama or Daddy would start praying. I started counting seconds—*one thousand one, one thousand two, one thousand three,* and so on.

In about fifteen seconds Carl said, " 'God be merciful unto us, and bless us; and cause his face to shine upon us; that thy way may be known upon earth, thy saving health among all nations. Let the people praise thee, O God; let all the people praise thee.' "

As I've said, Carl had reached the point where he wasn't going to prayer band too often, but it was good to see that he still remembered those few verses from the Psalms, verses that were very appropriate.

When Carl finished, I started counting, but not very long. In about three seconds Mama came on, singing the Lord's Prayer. Her voice was soft and clear, seeming to rise all around us from the ground there in the moonlight. It was the first time I'd ever heard her sing that. In fact, I had never even heard her recite the Lord's Prayer.

As soon as she finished, I started saying privately to God that Daddy was the tough one, he was the one that God would have to work mightily in order to shake. I hoped and hoped, waiting for God's power to act. But the seconds went by. Then I knew it wouldn't work. Even though Mr. Godbold must have waited almost a full minute, Daddy didn't say anything.

Finally Mr. Godbold prayed, softly but strongly, "Therefore I say unto you, whatsoever things you desire, when you pray, believe and you shall receive them. And when you stand praying, forgive, if you have anything against others, that your Heavenly Father may also forgive you your trespasses." Then he thanked God very specifically about the saving of the little baby. He asked for God's blessings on us who were about to drive in that black Plymouth to Jackson. Finally he closed by reciting from the 103rd Psalm:

" 'The Lord is merciful and gracious, slow to anger, and plenteous in mercy. He will not always chide: neither will he keep his anger forever. He hath not dealt with us after our sins; nor rewarded us according to our iniquities. For as the heaven is high above the earth, so great is his mercy toward them that fear him. As far as the east is from the west, so far hath he removed our transgressions from us. Like as a father pitieth his children, so the Lord pitieth them that fear him. For he knoweth our frame; he remembereth that we are dust.' "

The thought flashed through me like the pain from a burned finger that we were all dust: Floyd in his casket, Daddy bent sweating to reach for another brick, Mama with her hands moving over the piano, Carl with a newspaper figuring out ballplayers' batting averages, and Geraldine with her legs spraddled on the ground with that hair-patch pointed toward the sky.

" 'As for man, his days are as grass; as a flower of the field, so he flourisheth. For the wind passeth over it, and it is gone; and the place thereof shall know it no more. But the mercy of the Lord is from everlasting to everlasting upon them that fear him, and his righteousness unto children's children.' "

When he finished we picked our way through the grass and weeds without a word, back to the car. He shook all our hands, but nobody said anything to break the silence, like some kind of trance that we were all in. When Mama started the car, he raised his hand to wave but said nothing. We waved back. Then

Mama headed the car into the little white road back to the dark gravel again.

The gravel banged loud under the fenders of the Plymouth as Mama drove with a kind of hard quietness toward the south. Before us in the moonlight the road sometimes would twist away into the darkness of trees that seemed like nowhere.

It was at least five minutes before anybody said anything. Mama looked at Daddy for a second, then said, "Don't tell me, Carl, that you don't remember one single Bible verse you could have said?"

"I remember plenty of Bible verses. I've forgot more Bible verses than you ever read."

"Don't tell me that," Mama said, sniffing almost as loud as that dog Simon. "I led the choir for four years in Inverness. Before I met you and got married I was in church every Sunday."

As though he'd suddenly remembered, Daddy reached into his shirt pocket and brought out the Roi Tan cigar he'd been carrying in that pocket all afternoon. He peeled the cellophane and then bit the cigar end off and flicked it out the window. Leaning forward so the wind wouldn't blow the match out, he lighted the cigar. The smoke stirred strong and good through the car.

"It's a pity," he said slowly, "that you're not still back in Inverness, Clara, leading that choir."

Mama seemed to pay no attention to him. She looked ahead at the road, shaking her head from side to side. "Such a tiny baby, Carl. That was the tiniest baby I ever saw. Just think—someday that little thing will be a grown person."

Daddy puffed his cigar. "That's a pity too."

She said, "My God, Carl, couldn't you at least say something instead of standing there looking at the ground?"

"I'm not like you. I can't sing—not even the Lord's Prayer."

"You could have said the words—especially after I refreshed your mind by singing them."

"I'm still not like you," Daddy said. "I'm no hypocrite."

"Hypocrite? Hypocrite, for God's sake! The Lord knows I practice what I preach." She swung her head toward us in the back for a second. "Mark. Carl Junior. Do you think your mama's a hypocrite?"

Carl said, "No, I wouldn't call you that, Mama."

I said, "We have all sinned and fallen short—"

"Do you think I'm a hypocrite, Mark?"

"No, Mama. No more than I am."

She kind of tapped her hands on the steering wheel and glanced at Daddy. "Carl, someday when you're in Hell and I'm in Heaven you're going to look at me across that great gulf like that rich man looking up at the beggar. You're going to ask the Lord to send me down with a glass of cold water for you."

"I don't think so," Daddy said. "But if you do make the trip don't bring water. Make it a nice frosty Falstaff."

I said, "Daddy, you acted fine back there with Mr. Godbold. Please don't spoil it all by making fun now."

Mama said, "The beer talk reminds me, Carl. Where's the twenty dollars we decided to hold back on the boys' bill? We need things at the house, and I don't intend for you to buy beer with that money."

Daddy reached into his trousers pocket, took out a bill, and laid it on the front seat between them. Mama dropped her right hand down to get the money. Then she stuck it close to the light from the dashboard.

She said, "Oh, no you don't pull any such trick, Carl Torrance. This is just a ten. Where's the other one?"

"I left it on top of that little baby's bed."

Mama glanced at him for a second or two. Then I saw in her face that she believed him. She said, "Carl, you're the craziest man that ever lived. You're sure going to be a long time without beer this month."

"That's all right," Daddy said. "There's plenty of months I've been a long time without."